COME
TUMBLING
DOWN

SEANAN McGUIRE

A TOM DOHERTY ASSOCIATES BOOK

NEW YORK

COME TUMBLING DOWN

Copyright © 2019 by Seanan McGuire

All rights reserved.

Interior illustrations by Rovina Cai

A Tor.com Book
Published by Tom Doherty Associates
120 Broadway
New York, NY 10271

www.tor.com

Tor® is a registered trademark of Macmillan Publishing Group, LLC.

The Library of Congress Cataloging-in-Publication Data
is available upon request.

ISBN 978-0-7653-9931-1 (hardcover)
ISBN 978-0-7653-9930-4 (ebook)

Our books may be purchased in bulk for promotional, educational, or business use. Please contact your local bookseller or the Macmillan Corporate and Premium Sales Department at 1-800-221-7945, extension 5442, or by email at MacmillanSpecialMarkets@macmillan.com

First Edition: January 2020

Printed in the United States of America

0 9 8 7 6 5 4 3 2 1

FOR JILLIAN, WHO WOULD RECOGNIZE THE MOORS.
THEY WILL ALWAYS BE WAITING TO WELCOME YOU HOME.

I am what I am, and there's much about me that won't be changed with any amount of wishing or wanting. I'm sorry for that. I'd trade a great deal to share an afternoon in the hay with you, dust in the air and sweat on our skins and neither of us caring. But I'm afraid the experience would drive me mad. I am a creature of sterile environments. It's too late for me to change.

—JACK WOLCOTT

PART I

THE GRAVITY OF THE MOMENT

HOME AGAIN

ELEANOR WEST WAS FOND of saying—inasmuch as she was fond of saying anything predictable, sensible, or more than once—that her school had no graduates, only students who found somewhere else to do their learning for a time. Once a wayward child, always a wayward child. The school's doors would always be open; the lost and the lonely would always be welcome, whenever they wanted to come home.

When children were given into her keeping, the teachers she employed taught them about math and literature and science, according to the state's curriculum, and Eleanor herself taught them other, equally important things. She taught them how to lie and dissemble, and how to recognize the difference between the two. She taught them how to pick a lock and how to break a window, and any number of other skills that could be useful to someone who might, at any moment, need to drop everything and run for an impossible door, an impossible future, an impossible dream.

And really, that was her true gift to them: she taught them how to keep hoping in the face of a world that told them their memories were delusions, their lived experiences were lies, and their dreams were never going to come true. Perhaps that was her secret for engendering loyalty in a student body that was otherwise disinclined to trust adults, listen to them, or answer when they called. She *believed*.

For people like her students—people like Eleanor herself—belief was the rarest gift of all.

The parents of those students called her many things, when they were asked. "Kind," or "considerate," or "eccentric, in a way that makes sense for someone who works with children." Not many people asked. The children Eleanor sought for her school were, by and large, the sort whose parents wanted them swept away as quickly and quietly as possible. They had already disappeared once, only to come back . . . changed. So let them disappear again, this time with the proper paperwork in place. Let them go and hope that if they happened to come home a second time, they'd come back the way they'd been, and not the way that they'd become.

Hope is a vicious beast. It sinks in its claws and it doesn't let go. But Eleanor loved all her children, however wild they became, and most of them—the ones who were still capable of loving anyone in the strange, cruel world where they'd been born, where they feared they'd eventually die—loved her. At Eleanor West's Home for Wayward Children, they could let themselves breathe. They could be protected, for a time.

No solicitation. No visitors.

No quests.

1 WRAPPED IN LIGHTNING, WEEPING THUNDER

IT WAS OBVIOUS to anyone with a discerning eye that the school had started out as the country home of a family with more money than sense. The shape of the original architecture was still there, buried under newer construction. It had been a modest three-story home, once upon a renovation, but it had been embellished over the course of generations by widows and widowers who had handled their grief and their inheritance in the same manner: by picking up a hammer and setting to work.

The house had grown like a garden, sprouting wings and tower rooms and greenhouses as if they were nothing more consequential than mushrooms after a rain. What it had been was gone, reduced to nothing but a faint echo in the shape of a door or the structure of an awning. Its replacement was a delightfully rambling sprawl of porches and doors, dormer windows and inexplicable chimneys. Some of the tower rooms stood higher than the attic; some of the lower windows had been painted shut to keep them from flooding the halls every time it rained.

Still, lights could be seen at all levels of the school, both day and night, and the rooms were often filled with laughter. There were worse things for a house to hold.

The school stood alone in the middle of a vast, rolling field, which was dotted with copses of trees; there were no neighbors for miles in any direction. Eleanor had inherited the property upon the deaths of her parents, and had immediately tasked the family accountant with managing the bulk of her assets, giving him strict instructions to watch the land around hers for any signs of a sale. When he found those signs, he was to step in whenever possible to keep that land from going to market. No price was too dear to pay for privacy. Sometimes even she wasn't sure how much of the surrounding countryside she owned.

That still wasn't enough for some of her students. They sought deeper shadows, darker spaces, more privacy and freedom from the outside world. For those children, the basement was the most coveted real estate in the house, and its occupants defended it fiercely from suggestion of roommates or relocation.

On the hot summer night where we begin, the basement's occupant was a boy named Christopher. He was in his late teens and knew that, one way or another, his tenure at the school was nearing its natural end. Either he'd graduate and go home to parents who expected him to be interested in college, a career, what they called "the real world," or he'd find a door of latticed bone and butterfly wings, interlaced with marigold petals, and he'd disappear for a second, and final, time. He knew which ending he wanted.

He knew he didn't get to choose.

Maybe that's why he was stretched out on his bed like a corpse prepared for autopsy, with his hands folded across his chest and his fingers wrapped loosely around a flute carved from a single bone. There were no holes, only indentations etched into its surface, but something about its shape made its purpose perfectly clear.

The single small basement window was open, letting a breeze whisper through. The glass was dark and leaded, letting little light inside. Christopher didn't mind. He could always go outside when he wanted to feel the sun on his face. Most of his free time was spent in the grove behind the school, perched in the high branches and playing silent songs on his flute.

Sometimes the skeletal bodies of local wildlife— squirrels and rats and, on one surprising occasion, a deer—would rise from their unmarked graves and dance for him. When that happened, Christopher would lead them away from the school and pipe them to their final rest in a place no one would stumble across by mistake. It was weird how much some of his fellow students disliked bones, but whatever. He wouldn't have liked *their* worlds either, and it wasn't like they went out of their way to cover his clothes with glitter or rainbows or other reminders of their lost fairytale dreams. Keeping the grounds free of skeletal surprises seemed like the least he could do.

Sometimes being the last person on campus whose door had led to a world most of the student body dismissed as "creepy" really sucked. It hadn't been like that when he'd first arrived. Back then he'd shared the "creepy" designation with the Wolcott twins, who'd traveled together to the Moors—a world arguably even creepier than his own Mariposa—and had gone back to their heart's chosen home the same way.

Jack would have appreciated his skeleton dancers. Jack *had* appreciated his skeleton dancers, on the rare occasions when she'd been able to take her eyes off Jill long enough to see what he was doing. Jill had always been the more dangerous, less predictable Wolcott, for all that she was the one who dressed in pastel colors and lace and sometimes remembered that people liked it when you smiled. Something about the way she'd wrapped her horror movie heart in ribbons and bows had reminded him of a corpse that hadn't been properly embalmed, like she was pretty on the outside and rotten on the inside. Terrifying and subtly wrong.

Jack had been a monster, too: she'd just been more honest about it. She'd never tried to hide what she was, from anyone. The world they'd found on the other side of their door had made monsters of them both.

Jill had always talked about the Moors like a treasured toy, something she could polish and plunder as she saw fit. Jack had always talked about them with a wistful wildness in her eyes, like they were the most beautiful place she could imagine, so incredible she didn't know quite how to put it into words. Jill had been terrifying. Jack had been . . . familiar.

Sometimes Christopher thought any chance he'd had of falling for a girl with ordinary things like "skin" and "muscle tissue" and "a pulse" had ended with the soft, moist sound of Jack driving a pair of scissors through her sister's horrible heart. He could have loved her in that moment, *had* loved her when she'd pulled the scissors free and used them to cut a hole in the wall of the world. She'd called her door out of nothingness, out of sororicide and hope, and she'd carried her sister's body through it, into the bleeding light of a crimson moon.

He'd seen the Moors spreading out around her like a mother's arms, welcoming their wayward daughter home. Sometimes he still saw them when he closed his eyes at night. And then the door had slammed, and the Wolcott sisters had been gone, and he'd been left behind. He'd hated her for having the chance to go home, and he'd loved her for taking it without looking back or hesitating, and his fate, such as it was, had been sealed. If

Jack could go home, so could he. All he had to do was figure out *how*.

He ran his fingers along the surface of his flute, caressing it. When he closed his eyes, he could almost see the Skeleton Girl sitting next to him, clapping her opaline hands, delighted by his artistry. He could almost touch her.

The overhead light flickered as he was raising the flute to his mouth. He paused, looking at it quizzically. It flickered again before spitting a great, uneven bolt of lightning that struck the concrete floor with a crack so loud it was like the whole world was being broken.

Christopher had survived quite a few things in his seventeen years, from public school to cancer to a stint in a world peopled entirely by sentient, animate skeletons. He rolled to the side before the echoes of the crack had faded, pressing himself against the wall and hopefully out of the path of any further impossible lightning strikes. Not that "impossible" meant much around here. One of his closest friends was a temporarily bipedal mermaid; another was the crown prince of a goblin kingdom, and yet another was technically a candy construct brought back to life by a sort of demigoddess with a really large oven. Judging things based on their possibility wasn't a good way to stay alive.

It certainly wouldn't have worked in this case. Wide-eyed, Christopher watched another bolt of lightning lance down from the ceiling. It was followed by another, and another, until the air crackled with ozone and his hair stood on end and the floor was blackened and charred from successive impacts.

The door to the basement slammed open. A girl with blue and green hair rushed inside and started down the stairs, stopping halfway. Her eyes went terribly round as she stared at the lightning. It ignored her, continuing to draw a hot white line down the center of the room.

"Cora!" shouted Christopher. "Stay *exactly where you are*!" Lightning was attracted to tall things, right? As long as she wasn't the tallest thing in the room, she'd be safe.

It was also supposed to be attracted to metal, but it was hitting the floor, not the metal shelves against the wall or Jack's old autopsy table. Christopher had draped a tablecloth over the table, making it a little less obviously morbid, but was that enough to discourage lightning? And lightning usually came out of the sky, not out of the ceiling. Why should he assume anything about this lightning was going to behave normally?

"What's going on?" Cora had to yell to be heard. The air was so charged with static that her hair was frizzing and rising up from her shoulders. Under other circumstances, it might have been funny. At the moment, it was sort of terrifying. "We heard the noise all the way upstairs!"

The word "we" was worrisome. It could mean more people rushing into the basement, and hence into the striking radius of the lightning.

Of course, most of the students thought Christopher was a creepy freak, since he carried one of his bones around outside of his body, and had gone to a world populated by living, laughing, dancing skeletons, and voluntarily lived in the basement. So maybe Cora was the only one in hearing range who cared enough to check on him. He wasn't sure he liked that idea any more than he liked the thought of half the school getting electrocuted on his stairs, but hey, what was life without a few contradictions?

"I don't know!" he yelled. "It just started *happening*!"

"Maybe you blew a fuse?"

Despite the gravity of the situation, Christopher paused to stare at Cora. She looked blankly back, her technicolor hair continuing to rise farther and farther into the electrically charged air.

"That's not how fuses *work*!" he shouted.

"Do you have a *better* idea?"

He didn't. Which was a problem, given the circumstances. Another bolt of lightning struck the floor, followed by another, and another, until the afterimages swimming behind his eyes were so heavy and bright that he could barely see the room.

Then it stopped.

Cora and Christopher stared at the blackened spot. The light fixture seemed undamaged, which was probably impossible, but was also less important than getting out of the basement before the lightning started again. Christopher sat up, cautiously stretching one foot toward the floor.

The lightning resumed. Cora squeaked, not quite a gasp and not quite a scream, but something small and shrill and laughable. Christopher wasn't laughing. He was watching as the lightning came down faster and faster, forming crackling chains of light. There was something *behind* that light, something buried in the brightness, something clean and old and unfamiliar, something—

With a final great sheet of blue-white brilliance, the lightning stopped again. The air, still heavy with ozone, pulsed under the weight of what it had just birthed.

And there, in the center of the room, atop the blackened concrete, was a door.

It would have been an ordinary door if it hadn't been standing where no door was normally found, where no wall was present to support it. Christopher slid shakily off the bed and stood, keeping his eyes on the door the whole time.

"Cora?" he called. "You see this?"

"It's a door." She finished making her way down the stairs, clutching the bannister, hair still bushed-out and frizzy. "There isn't usually a door there."

"I think I would have noticed, yeah."

"Is it . . . ?" The question died on her lips, like she was afraid speaking her suspicions out loud would stop them from being true.

Christopher shook his head. "No. My door didn't—I mean, Mariposa isn't big on lightning. The Country of Bones runs on a different kind of power. This isn't my door. Is it yours?"

"I didn't have a door." Cora moved toward him with exquisite care, skirting the char marks on the floor. Sometimes it surprised him how delicately she could move. She was a large, round glory of a girl, and between her size and her hair, it seemed like she should take up more space than she actually did. "I had a patch of water-weeds and a pattern of light on the water. Miss Eleanor says that's pretty common for submerged worlds. Wood rots, steel rusts, but abstract concepts remain."

"Sometimes all this gives me a headache," said Christopher. He took a cautious step toward the door. It stayed where it was, apparently solid, and didn't burst into flames, or strike him with a bolt of electricity, or anything else unfriendly.

"Do you want me to get Kade?"

Christopher hesitated. Kade was Eleanor's nephew and recognized second-in-command: when something didn't necessarily need the attention of the headmistress, it was Kade who made everything work. But classes had ended hours ago, and he was probably upstairs in the attic, working on his own projects. He didn't get much time to himself, what with the little problems that cropped up during the day and managing the school's shared wardrobe.

"No," said Christopher slowly. "I don't want to bother him just yet."

Cora eyed him. "It's a *door*."

"I can see that."

"Most of this school is waiting for a door."

"I am aware."

"So don't you think—"

"I don't *know*, okay? I've never had a door appear in the middle of my bedroom before! And it's all lightning and old oak, and that sounds like Jack and Jill, but they left before you got here and they're not coming back, so I don't know whose door this could possibly be. It doesn't make sense. I need a second to think. Let me think!"

Cora blinked before she said, in a stiff tone, "I'm just trying to make sure we stay safe."

Christopher took a deep breath. "I'm sor—"

That was as far as he got before the rusted doorknob began shaking, like something was fighting it. Christopher and Cora exchanged a glance. Then, in unison, they took a single long step back, away from whatever was about to come through. Neither of them ran.

The doorknob twisted.

The door shuddered in its frame, which seemed to shift and sigh, like it was letting go of some unspoken expectation.

The door swung inward.

The girl standing on the other side looked to be in her late teens, broad-shouldered and heavy, dressed in an

old-fashioned homespun dress. There was a stained apron tied around her waist. A twisted scar crawled up one side of her neck and crossed her cheek in a flat white line, vanishing behind the honeyed waves of her hair. She probably thought of that hair as her best feature: it was thick and glossy and beautiful in a way her pallid skin wasn't.

Lightning crashed behind her, both illuminating her and throwing the bundle in her arms into sudden, terrible relief.

It was another girl, slighter, smaller, long and lithe of limb. She was as pale as her companion, although not as gray around the edges, and she hung in the first girl's arms like a body prepared for burial. She wore a gown of white, frothing lace, and her pale hair dangled, long and unbound, like the flag of some dead nation.

Christopher gasped. For a moment, he couldn't breathe. He grasped for something to hold him upright and found Cora, who stood solidly under his clutching fingers and didn't make a sound.

"Jack?" he asked. "Jill?"

The stranger, her arms laden with the unnamed Wolcott twin, didn't say a word as she stepped across the threshold. The door slammed shut behind her. There was another blue-white flash as it vanished, leaving the four teens alone at the bottom of the school, standing in the afterimage, unsure of what was meant to happen next.

2 THEY ALWAYS COME BACK HOME

CHRISTOPHER SUCKED IN a sharp breath, almost choking when the ozone-laden air hit the back of his throat. Coughing, he focused on the girl carrying the unconscious—dead? No, unconscious, surely nothing in the Moors would *dare* harm a Wolcott—twin.

"I'm sorry," he said. "I don't know who you are. Is that Jack or Jill? Is she hurt?"

It had to be Jill. Her hair was sleek and glossy and looked like it had been brushed a thousand times a day for the last ten years. Jack's hair had never been that well-cared-for. More importantly, the girl's wrists were thin and delicate. The muscle of Jack's arms and shoulders had always been the most obvious distinction between her and her sister. She'd worn long-sleeved shirts with buttoned cuffs, but it had always been clear that one of them did physical labor and one of them . . . didn't.

Probably-Jill somehow managed to look moonwashed

even in the electric glare of the basement light. She was wearing a lacy, diaphanous nightgown. It was elaborate enough that Christopher was pretty sure he was supposed to call it something pretentious, like a "peignoir," and it was cut to show an uncomfortable amount of her too-pale skin. Despite all that, the collar was high enough to brush her jaw and so thick with lace rosettes that he couldn't tell how much scar tissue it concealed. Perfect for a vampire's adopted daughter.

The stranger opened her mouth, working it soundlessly for several seconds before closing it and shaking her head.

"I'll get help," said Cora, turning and running up the stairs before Christopher could ask her not to.

Honestly, he wasn't even able to quite formulate the reasons why he would've objected. Maybe it was the ozone in the air, the charged feeling of something getting ready to break down or break through or break to pieces around them. He was a student at a school for kids who'd traveled between worlds, crossing thresholds that should have been uncrossable; for something to feel *strange* to him, it had to be pretty extreme.

The Wolcott—Jill, it had to be Jill—in the stranger's arms remained pale and motionless. Christopher frowned.

"Do you want to put her down?" he asked. "My name's Christopher. I was a friend of Jack's before she went back to the Moors. I mean, not really. Jack doesn't have friends, she has minions who haven't figured out their place in the grand scheme of things. But she liked me okay, and Jill tolerated me, and this used to be their room. You could put her on my bed if you wanted to."

The stranger shook her head again, looking frustrated. Her mouth moved.

"I'm sorry. I can't—if you're making any sort of sound, I can't hear it."

The stranger took a deep breath and mouthed something, lips moving slowly and deliberately. Christopher blinked.

"Too soft?" he asked. "Is that what you're saying, the bed is too soft?"

The stranger nodded.

Christopher gestured toward the autopsy table. With the tablecloth draped over it, it barely even looked like a place where people took dead bodies apart. "Jack used to sleep there. She said it was better for her back. I mean, she also said she could extract someone else's spine and give herself a new back if necessary, but it seemed like a lot of work. Better to go straight for proper lumbar support."

The stranger mouthed the words "Thank you" and moved toward the table. She gave the cloth a quizzical look, shrugged, and lay Jill down with exquisite care, stretching out her legs and folding her hands over her chest in a classically funereal pose.

Jill's hair seemed to stymie the stranger. She started to tug it straight, then stopped, looking at it like she'd

never seen it before. Finally, she stepped back, burying
her hands in the folds of her skirt, and gave Christopher
a silent, worried look.

"I'm sorry," he said. "I don't know what's wrong,
but I'm still sorry. Is she . . ." He stopped. If Jill wasn't
breathing, he didn't want to know about it.

"Holy hell, is that *Jill*?"

Christopher turned toward the stairs, untensing. Kade
would know what to do. Kade always knew what to do. It
was one of his best, and most irritating, qualities.

Kade wasn't alone on the stairs. Sumi was behind
him, bouncing onto her toes and straining to see over his
shoulder. Frustrated, she planted her hands at the small
of Kade's back and pushed.

"Come *on*, come *on*, there's adventure in the air and
you're *too slow*!"

"I don't think that's adventure so much as it's static,
Sumi; calm down," said Kade. He took the remainder
of the stairs in four long, lanky steps, hopping down the
final three in his hurry to get to the silent Wolcott.

He had almost reached her when the stranger stepped
between them, glaring down at him. He stopped where
he was. Sumi peeked around him at the other girl.

"You're not tall, but you walk like you are," she said
approvingly. "I've always said we needed more mountains around here. We're not going to hurt Jack. We're
her friends. Or we were, anyway, before I died and she
left. You know how that is."

To Christopher's surprise, the stranger smiled and made a see-sawing motion with her hand, apparently agreeing with Sumi.

"That's not Jack," said Kade. "That's Jill. Look at her hands."

"Jack's still Jack when she's not wearing gloves," said Sumi. "She's still Jack when she's not wearing her own skin, too. It's a neat trick. Imagine if I could put on someone else's skin and have everyone believe it was really them! I'd be so many people every day."

"Sumi . . ." Kade pinched the bridge of his nose before addressing the stranger. "I apologize for my friend. She went to a Nonsense world, and it left her a little scrambled."

"Dying scrambled me more," said Sumi matter-of-factly. She stepped around Kade, heading for the velvet curtain covering the basement's rear wall. "There's an easy way to answer this. We'll wake her up and ask *her* who she thinks she is. If I'm right and it's Jack, you owe me extra dessert."

"You always get extra dessert," said Christopher. "I think you have syrup in your veins."

"If only," chirped Sumi. She twitched the curtain aside, revealing the jars and vials and beakers full of dangerous chemicals Jack had left behind when she departed.

"What's Sumi doing?" asked Cora, from beside Christopher's left elbow.

"What the fu— Don't *do* that!" he exclaimed, whipping around to stare at her. "When did you get here?"

Cora shrugged. "Kade and Sumi were arguing about who the girl on the table is. I don't know her either way, so I figured I'd be quiet."

"I swear I'm going to *bell* you," muttered Christopher. Secretly, he was grateful. Cora being too quiet and sneaking up on him was normal. Sumi being weird was normal. Strangers carrying maybe-dead girls appearing in his room was not normal. The air smelling of ozone was not normal.

A little normalcy was a good thing. Especially when Sumi was turning away from the shelves with a vial of something yellow and viscous in her hand and a manic look in her eye. Even Kade looked nervous.

"What are you going to do, Sumi?"

"Ask and answer," she said brightly, and started for Jill. Before she reached her target, she stopped, looking at the stranger, and said, "I'm not going to hurt her. Unless she labeled her own things wrong, and if she did that, I think it's less me hurting her and more her learning some important lessons about lab safety. All right?"

The stranger frowned, making a sharp gesture with one hand.

Unexpectedly, Sumi lit up. "Oh!" she said. "You sign! Well, that makes this easier. I swear on the candy corn fields and the strawberry sea that I wouldn't ever hurt her on *purpose*. Accidents happen to the best of us. But

I don't think anything can start happening until she's awake, and that means you need to let me. Please?"

The stranger sighed, broad shoulders sagging, and stepped aside.

"Thank you," said Sumi. Her smile was gentler than Christopher had ever known it to be, a momentary tenderness that was quickly undone when she popped the vial of mysterious yellow fluid open and shoved it under the motionless Wolcott twin's nose.

"It's Jill," said Christopher.

"No, it's not," said Sumi.

The Wolcott's eyes snapped open and she jerked upright, taking a huge, shuddering breath before starting to cough. She raised her hands toward her mouth and froze, staring at them. Something about her own fingers seemed to horrify her. Her eyes went wider and wider until she started coughing again, harder this time. She didn't cover her mouth. She didn't seem able to finish the motion.

"She's having a panic attack," said Kade. "Sumi, you need to back off *right now*."

"No, I don't," said Sumi. "Jack, it's me. Look, I stopped being dead. Resurrections make you happy, right? Behold the power of science!"

The stranger stepped around Sumi, putting a heavy hand on the Wolcott's shoulder. The girl huddled against her, coughs slowly stopping, only to be replaced by a sharp keening noise.

"I have no idea what's going on," said Cora.

"That makes two of us," said Kade.

The stranger stroked the twin's head with her free hand. The smaller girl huddled even closer, pressing her face into the stranger's apron. It did nothing to dull the razor edge of her keening.

"It's Jack." Sumi dropped the vial on the table before scrubbing her palms against her jeans. "I don't know how it's Jack, but it's Jack. I don't know who her friend is, either, but I know she's been dead before, so we're both members of a really lousy club that most people never get to join. I know a not-dead girl wouldn't be here with Jack unless it was really, really important."

Kade started to reply, then hesitated. Sumi had been dead when Jack and Jill left for the Moors, but she'd known them well enough to know that neither Wolcott would have voluntarily come back. Like most of Eleanor's students, they'd dreamt of nothing but returning to their true, beloved home since the day they were enrolled.

"You said she signs," said Kade. "What does that mean, exactly?"

"Means she talks with her hands," said Sumi. "I don't speak the same dialect, but I guess the Moors never developed their own sign language, because what she's said so far looks like ASL, the way ASL would look if you never left your farm to make sure you weren't experiencing linguistic drift."

Sumi's perpetual sugar buzz and gleeful ridiculousness could make it easy to forget how smart she was.

Kade nodded slowly. Then he turned to the stranger. "Can you understand me? If you can, will you please tell Sumi why you're here?"

Sumi scoffed. "She can *hear*. She just can't make *sounds*. Don't act like she's stupid."

The stranger looked uncertain, maybe because of the Wolcott still clinging to her side. Sumi sighed as she turned to the pair and began moving her hands, fingers flashing and darting with incredible speed. Even silent, Sumi somehow managed to be loud enough to fill the entire room.

"What are you saying?" asked Kade.

"Girl talk," said Sumi. "Pure nonsense. None of your business." She kept signing.

Finally, slowly, the stranger took her hand away from the Wolcott's hair. The Wolcott whimpered and burrowed closer, pressing her face deeper into the stranger's apron. The stranger started signing, more slowly than Sumi—which wasn't saying much. Some hummingbirds were slower than Sumi.

Sumi wasn't moving now. She was watching, eyes sharp, expression sharper, occasionally interjecting a rapidly signed reply. Finally, she nodded. "It's nice to meet you, Alexis," she said, and looked to Kade. An unforgiving coldness had settled over her in the last few moments, a coldness befitting a girl who'd saved a world, and died, and risen again, all before she had the chance to turn eighteen.

Eleanor West's Home for Wayward Children was an island of misfit toys, a place to put the unfinished stories and the broken wanderers who could butcher a deer and string a bow but no longer remembered what to do with indoor plumbing. It was also, more importantly, a holding pen for heroes. Whatever they might have become when they'd been cast out of their chosen homes, they'd been heroes once, each in their own ways. And they did not forget.

"Her name is Alexis," said Sumi, voice artificially calm. "She's here because she hopes we can help Jack; because she doesn't think anyone else can."

"So that is Jack, then," said Kade.

"Yes, and no," said Sumi. "This is Jack, but she's in Jill's body. Jill stole hers and ran away with it."

There was a pause as everyone took this in. Finally, faintly, Cora said, "Oh. Is that all?"

3 WINDOWS OF THE SOUL

KADE YANKED THE wardrobe open and started digging through its contents, scattering clothes in all directions. Sumi perched atop a nearby stack of books, watching him. He grabbed a waistcoat, discarded it, and reached for a vest, muttering about whipstitches and adjustable clips. Sumi cocked her head.

"Why is it so important for you to find something that fits her, when she's still wailing and crying and snotting all over everything?" she asked. "You call *me* the nonsensical one, but right now it feels like you're putting the frosting before the fire."

"Clothes matter," he said, draping the vest over his arm and reaching for a pile of neatly folded blouses. "Clothes are part of how you learn to feel like yourself, and not someone who just happens to look like you. Don't you remember what it was like when someone else decided what you were going to wear?"

Sumi shuddered—not as theatrically as she normally would have. This wasn't something to be seen. It was something she felt all the way down to her bones, which were the only remaining part of her original body.

"My parents," she said. "They were like Nancy's but the other way around, chasing monochrome instead of spectrums. They didn't understand. Thought if they threw enough gray and gray and gray at me, I'd forget I'd seen rainbows and learn how to be their little sparrowgirl again. She died in Confection and I rose from her ashes, a pretty pastry phoenix. I need my color. It keeps me breathing when I see me in the mirror at midnight."

"Exactly." Kade slung a measuring tape around his neck and grabbed a stack of charcoal trousers. "Jack is *literally* in someone else's body. That's got to be like dysphoria squared. She's scared and confused and she needs to be anchored. Get that shoe box for me, would you?"

Sumi picked up the box. "Is it full of bees?"

Kade eyed her. "I don't want to know why you think I'd have a box of bees up here. No, it's not full of bees. It's full of gloves. Jack's gloves. Jill always had less muscle mass than her sister, so I'm guessing I'll need to do some alterations on the rest of her clothing if I want it to fit her correctly, but the gloves? Those should be fine."

"That will help," said Sumi, looking approvingly at the box. "Jack doesn't like it when the world touches her."

"I know. Come on. I don't want you up here unsupervised."

Sumi dimpled, looking young and innocent and terribly dangerous all at the same time. "What could I possibly do that would be so awful?"

"Everything. Every moment of the day. Since you were born." Kade waited in the doorway until Sumi flounced past him, then closed the door as he followed her.

They'd have to involve Eleanor eventually. She liked it when the students were self-sufficient, and didn't believe in coddling them; after all, they'd seen wonders beyond their apparent ages, had fought monsters and saved kingdoms. Surely they could go about their business without being smothered by the nearest available adult. She'd still want to know that Jack was back, and that something terrible had happened in the Moors. She'd want to *help*.

Or she would have, once. Eleanor had been less and less invested in the daily operation of the school since Lundy's death. All the current teachers were adults who thought they worked at some sort of strange boarding school for the children of eccentric hippies: they didn't know about the doors, or the wonders they concealed. Eleanor continued to handle student intake, and had taken over Lundy's daily therapy sessions, but she was slipping.

Eleanor had started the school because she didn't want other children to suffer the way she'd suffered when she returned from her own Nonsense world and ran up against the disbelief of the people who should have been most willing to believe her. Strange as it was to consider, she'd been young once, quick and bright and flexible-minded, ready to handle any challenge . . . except for exile. So she'd opened a school, with the goal of getting it as stable as she could before senility softened her mind and she went back through her own door. Before she went home.

Kade had always assumed there'd be someone to take over when that happened. Not Lundy, maybe, whose own journeys had left her a brilliant woman trapped in a body growing younger every year, but someone adult and capable. Someone who'd understand why it was so important, and who'd be willing to keep Kade on, keep teaching him everything he'd need to know to eventually step up as headmaster. And of course, there was college to be considered, courses in education and business and . . .

And he wanted to involve Eleanor in this latest potential crisis, and he didn't want to involve her at all, because that theoretical adult had yet to appear. What if she decided this was the last thing she could handle? What if she left him, unprepared and alone, to take over running the school?

The thought made his heart beat too fast and his chest feel too tight. *Panic attacks aren't supposed to be contagious*, he thought sourly. If he went too far down the metaphorical rabbit hole, he'd need to take his binder off in order to get his breath back, and he wanted that even less than he wanted to talk to his great-aunt.

Sumi followed him down the stairs from the attic to the main floor and along the hallway toward the basement, uncharacteristically quiet. When they reached the basement door, she reached out and placed a long-fingered hand on his arm, stopping him.

"There's enough air for everyone," she said, voice soft. "No one's going to take it away from you."

"Weirdly enough, that helps," he said, because weirdly enough, it did. "Let's see if we can't convince Jack of the same thing."

The scene in Christopher's room hadn't changed much: Jack was still huddled against Alexis, the yellow tablecloth bunched up around her bare feet and calves. Christopher was standing a reasonable distance away, with Cora halfway hiding behind him, like she expected to be ejected from the room at any moment.

"Oh, this is *silly*," said Sumi. She shoved past Kade, taking back the box of gloves as she went, and hopped down the last six stairs, not pausing until she was next to Alexis. She slammed the box down on the table, creating a banging noise loud enough to make Jack flinch.

Sumi rolled her eyes.

"I know, I know, panic is fun, but sometimes revenge is better," she said. "Choose revenge. Choose better. I brought you gloves."

"They're yours," said Kade hastily. "I saved your clothes after you left. Most of them will need a little alteration, but no one else has ever worn them. Only you."

"Only . . . if I wear them now . . . someone else *is* wearing them." Jack's voice was cracked and unsteady: she sounded like she was teetering on the verge of some vast, unseen abyss. She turned her head, viewing the others through a bridal veil of loose blonde strands. "I don't know where she's been I don't *know* I *don't* know *I—*"

Sumi slapped her.

It wasn't a hard slap as such things went, but it was hard enough to echo through the room. Alexis stiffened, starting to step forward. Jack's hand against her arm stopped her. She looked at the smaller woman, expression questioning. Jack shook her head.

"No," she said. Then, more loudly, she repeated, "No. That was quite enough violence for one day. Thank you, Sumi. How is it you're not dead? Am I seeing ghosts? If that's a side effect of what's been done to me, I'm going to be even more displeased than I already am."

"Who talks like that?" muttered Cora. "And I realize this is far from the weirdest thing happening here, but Christopher, why do you have a metal table?"

"Technically, I don't," said Christopher. "It's Jack's. I mean, it belongs to her. I just put a tablecloth over it because it's creepy."

"A good autopsy table isn't *creepy*, it's *essential*," said

Jack. She squinted at him. "Christopher? Am I to assume this is your room now? Who's your verdigrised friend? I don't recognize the voice."

Seeming to relax for the first time since she'd carried Jack through the door, Alexis tapped her arm and signed something. Jack rolled her eyes.

"Of *course* I'm missing my glasses," she said. "My sister—may the Drowned Gods devour every scrap of meat clinging to her barnacled bones—stole them when she stole my *skull*. You're all quite blurry at any distance."

"I'm Cora and I'm very confused right now," said Cora.

"Then you clearly belong with this student body," said Jack. She leaned against Alexis as she pulled the box of gloves closer. "Have there been any other miraculous resurrections since my departure? I do like to keep up on the latest gossip."

"Everyone else who was dead is still dead, so far as I know," said Kade. "Nancy's door came back for her. She's gone to the Halls of the Dead."

"We left Nadya there when we went to find Sumi's ghost," said Christopher.

"Had the Halls of the Dead offended you in some way, that they deserved a Drowned Girl with no sense of etiquette?" Jack pulled out a pair of white kid gloves, shuddered, and set them aside, continuing to rummage through the remaining options.

"It was a trade," said Cora. "Sumi for Nadya." She

couldn't quite keep the bitterness out of her voice. Nadya had been her first and fiercest friend at the school. Sumi was . . .

Sumi was Sumi. Spending time with her was like trying to form a close personal relationship with a cloud of butterflies. Pretty—dazzling, even—but not exactly companionable. And some of the butterflies had knives, and that was where the metaphor collapsed.

"Fascinating." Jack pulled out another pair of gloves. These ones were black suede, and after a momentary examination, she tugged them methodically on, checking each finger to be sure the fit was close and snug.

Cora had never seen anyone put on a pair of gloves with such care. Jack's world seemed to narrow to nothing but herself, the gloves, and the need to make sure they covered her hands. When she was finally satisfied, she sighed and sagged against Alexis again, somehow sitting up straighter at the same time, like a doll with broken legs and a rigid spine.

"Alexis, these are my schoolmates, although one was dead by Jill's hand the last time I saw her—"

"Hi," chirped Sumi.

"—and one is a colorful stranger. Schoolmates, this is my betrothed, Miss Alexis Chopper, who shares the unfortunate distinction of having died at my sister's hand. She's currently unable to speak, but I assure you, she understands everything you say."

Alexis waved.

Jack switched her attention to Christopher. "Christopher, you've been occupying my room while I've been gone. Is it too much to hope that you've some of my things?"

"You're sitting on an autopsy table," said Christopher. "I kept everything."

"I suppose there are still mercies in the world." Jack closed her eyes. "If you look at the rack of red shelves, third from the top, there should be a small oak box. Inside, you'll find my spare glasses. I would be immensely grateful if you'd bring them here. I don't intend to send people questing for every individual part of a decent wardrobe, pleasant as the distraction would be, but I can't proceed with any clarity if I can't see who I'm talking to."

"Jack, what *happened*?" asked Kade. "You're not . . ."

"Supposed to be here? Quite myself?" Jack's laugh was low and bitter. "I suppose I should be grateful that my sister and I are identical twins, but it's not enough. I can feel the panic clawing at me, trying to bite through my bones. This body is . . . it's filthy. I need a thousand baths before I can even begin to feel like I might someday be clean again."

"Is it because you don't know where it's been?" asked Sumi.

Jack opened her eyes and favored the smaller girl with a withering look. "I can only dream of such glorious ignorance. My issue with *this* body is that I know precisely where it's been, precisely what it's done, and moreover, precisely what has been done to it. I am a ghost trapped in a charnel house, and I dislike it immensely."

Alexis began stroking Jack's hair. Jack reached up and caught her hand with gloved fingers, pulling it to her lips and kissing it gently.

"I'm sorry, love," she said. "I'm trying. For you, I'm trying."

Christopher blinked. Of all the things he'd been expecting—which, to be honest, included essentially none of the day's events—Jack showing affection toward another human being had *not* made the list. He turned and hurried across the room to the shelf Jack had identified, beginning to sift through its contents.

It was a little odd how he'd preserved all Jack's things, even after the room had officially become his. Nancy had taken it before him. She'd been newer to the school, but she'd been given priority by her roommate's death—even with as dotty as Eleanor could sometimes be, she'd been able to recognize that Nancy probably didn't want to sleep in Sumi's room without Sumi. It had been Nancy who'd cleaned out the twins' clothes, giving them to Kade to add to the school's communal wardrobe. She hadn't been there long enough to deal with anything else, and when Christopher moved in, he'd found the combination of mad scientist's lab and Victorian lady's parlor oddly soothing. It wasn't anything like Mariposa, but it wasn't anything like his parents' house, either. It was his. It was home.

Sure, he'd covered up the creepier aspects, since there was "willing to share space with a taxidermically preserved alligator" and then there was "waking up every morning and looking at a whole shelf of different kinds of acid." One was quaint. The other was disturbing.

The box was right where Jack had said it would be. Christopher picked it up, hesitated, and grabbed a pack of wipes. Jack liked to be clean. Jack took "liking to be clean" to the extreme. She'd want her glasses to be clean before she put them on.

Sumi and Alexis were signing to each other again when he returned to the group. "Here," he said, offering the box and wipes to Jack. "I thought you might want to clean the lenses."

"Normally, I'd say something about your clear inclination toward hoarding, but at the moment, I'm too grateful." Jack took the box and wipes, setting the latter aside before opening the former to reveal four pairs of wire-framed glasses nestled in a bed of velvet. She selected the first pair, held it in front of her eyes, winced, and reached for the second. "I'll just be a moment."

"Jill never wore glasses," said Kade.

"Jill was, perhaps, comforted by seeing the world wrapped in cotton fluff and stripped of hard edges," said Jack, discarding the second pair of glasses. "She's needed corrective lenses as long as I have. She simply lacked the incentive to wear them. Eye protection is of the utmost importance in the laboratory setting. I would have worn plain glass, had I not needed something more functional. Once the acid becomes airborne, it's no one's friend."

"Ah," said Kade. More gently, he began, "Jack, about your sister—"

"Not yet." Jack held the third pair of glasses up to her face, nodded, and reached for the cleaning cloths. "I'm remembering how to breathe. Please, be patient with me. Be patient with both of us. Although . . ." She caught Alexis's wrist, fingers expertly pinning down the other girl's pulse. "If we could take a moment for me to perform a quick restorative procedure for Alexis's benefit, I would be immensely grateful."

Alexis signed something. Sumi smirked.

"Your girlfriend says you're hot when you get all science-y," she reported.

"My girlfriend is a genius of incomparable scope and should be listened to in all things," said Jack. She slipped the glasses onto her face, pushing them up the bridge of her nose with one black-gloved finger until they were positioned perfectly. Then she sighed, the deep, satisfied sigh of someone who'd just seen the world come—quite literally—into focus. "Much better."

"Does that mean you're ready to tell us what happened?" asked Kade.

"A moment." Jack turned to Alexis, hands moving in a sharp, interrogative gesture.

Alexis motioned to Sumi, then turned her attention to Jack, her own hands beginning to move faster. There was no language barrier between them: they had clearly been communicating in this manner for some time. They had found a simple intimacy in sign, making it entirely their own. Sometimes they'd abandon signs in the middle of a gesture, their message already conveyed, language become shorthand become intuitive understanding.

It was beautiful and strange and it made Christopher's ears burn with something like jealousy, and something like longing, and something like regret. He'd been that close to someone, once. He would be again, if he could ever find the way to Mariposa.

If he could ever find his own way home.

Jack finally nodded to Alexis and put her hands against the autopsy table, scooting toward the edge. "I require two sets of jumper cables, an inversion circuit, one of the small generators I left in the closet, and several other items which I can collect myself. This body may have the strength of a wet kitten, but the day I can't manage to mix a batch of electrode gel unassisted is the day I abandon all hope of ever finding a solution."

Her bare feet hit the concrete floor. She stopped for a moment, shuddering again. Alexis moved to steady her. Jack held up one gloved hand, motioning for the other girl to keep her distance.

"No," she said softly. "I need to do this. Can you please . . . love, please get on the table and get yourself ready. This will go so much easier if I know you're all right before I begin."

Alexis signed something.

Jack shook her head. "No. *No.* You matter as much as I do. More, even. This body has only been resurrected once. It's delicate, but it's not fragile. Please get on the table."

Alexis nodded. Jack relaxed and started for the shelves. She was clearly still tense, and as jumpy as some strange wild creature, but she was moving like a girl on a mission.

Christopher glanced at Cora, who was watching with wide, bewildered eyes as Alexis pulled the cloth all the way off the autopsy table and dropped it on the floor. With this accomplished, Alexis climbed onto the table and stretched herself out, as quickly and easily as if this were the sort of thing she did every day.

"I'm so confused right now," Cora said.

"Welcome to the club," said Christopher.

"There's nothing confusing about it, except for maybe the part where you're not getting the generator and hauling it into position!" Jack grabbed several jars of differently colored liquids from the shelves. "Time is of the essence, in so many different directions. I require trousers, and a shower, and assistance in saving the Moors. You require the full story of what Alexis and I are doing here. The best way for all of us to get what we need is for you to *move that generator.*"

"Come on," said Christopher. "I know where she kept them."

"Is she always this demanding?" asked Cora, following him toward the closet. It was nice to have something to do; it made her feel less like she'd somehow stumbled into the audience of some Victorian penny dreadful, watching the story unfold but unable to influence it.

"Yeah," said Christopher, with unabashed fondness. "I mean, she sort of had to be. From everything she said, the Moors don't have a lot of patience for people being wishy-washy."

"That's the world she and her sister went to?"

"Yeah."

"Huh."

The generators, plural, were in the closet Jack had indicated, along with several cannisters of fuel. Cora eyed them with undisguised dismay.

"This is a fire hazard," she said. "And who needs *three* generators? Are these supposed to be for the whole school?"

"No, they're for private use, and I can hear you," called Jack.

Cora's face flared red. "Great," she mumbled.

Christopher touched her shoulder, expression concerned. "Hey," he said. "It's not you. That's just how she is. She doesn't mean anything by it. You know how mad scientists in movies are always muttering about showing those fools who laughed at them in the academy? Well, she's sort of like that, only crankier, because she didn't even get to *go* to the academy. Help me move one of these things."

Together, they were able to hoist the smallest of the three generators—which was deceptively heavy, and raised questions about how Jack had managed to get it down the stairs in the first place—and shuffle-walk it across the basement to the autopsy table. The tablecloth was gone. Alexis was stretched out with her hands by her sides, her temples, throat, wrists, and ankles glistening with conduction gel. Jack had located electrodes somewhere, applying them to Alexis's temples, throat, ankles, and the insides of her wrists; they were connected to wires that extended to the leading ends of both pairs of jumper cables. The wires were wrapped firmly around the clamps, forming two braided bridges between them and Alexis's body. As for the other end of the cables . . .

Cora stopped, nearly dropping her end of the generator. "*No,*" she said, with surprising strength. "I'm not going to help you—you can't—*no.* This isn't okay. You can't do this."

"Do what?" asked Jack, daintily wiping away a smear of conduction gel that had extended too far down Alexis's neck for her liking. "Science? Because I assure you, I can do all the science I like, and you won't be the first to try and stop me. I know what I'm doing. Please don't try to interfere."

"It's all right, Cora," said Kade soothingly. "Alexis is from the Moors."

Cora stared at him. "What is *that* supposed to mean?"

"It means she's dead," said Jack. Her voice remained

calm, like she was remarking on the weather. "My sister killed her, rather violently, I might add; my sister used these hands—" The veneer of calm broke, snapped cleanly in two, as Jack stopped talking and balled the hands in question into tight fists, her shoulders going hunched as she struggled to keep herself under control.

"It's all right," said Sumi. "A tool is only a weapon when it's held by people who want to use it the wrong way. Or maybe it's the other way around, I don't know, but you're not her. You're not."

"Muscle has memory all its own," said Jack. "Bodies remember what they've done. This body remembers . . . terrible things. Unspeakable things. What is she teaching *my* body, right now? I don't know. I am afraid. So *please*." She slammed her hands flat on the autopsy table, causing everyone but Alexis to jump. "Move my generator into place, and let me work. I am begging you. Do not allow me to debase myself for nothing."

"On it," said Christopher. He started moving again, leaving Cora with little choice but to follow or drop the generator on his feet. She followed.

Once the generator was in position, Jack began her final preparations. Slowly at first, then with increasing confidence as she adjusted clamps, checked wires, and finally verified that the generator was properly fueled. It was a sort of poetry, the way she shifted from task to task, the absolute assurance in her gestures. Finally, she leaned in and pressed a kiss to Alexis's lips.

"You'll be better in a moment, darling," she said, not seeming to care who was listening. She stepped back, and leaned down to put a finger on the generator switch. "Those of you who value your retinas, close your eyes."

Cora did, but not quite fast enough: the electric ghost of the lightning leaping off the generator danced behind her eyelids, haunting her. The sound of the generator's engine was big enough to fill the world, roaring and rampant.

Eyes still closed, she shouted, "Do generators always work like this?"

"Not just no, but *hell* no!" Kade shouted back. "Jack, if you break the school, I'm telling my aunt on you!"

"Calm down, you unimaginative, unscientific fool. Everything is going according to plan." The sound of lightning striking flesh, very close by, punctuated Jack's declaration, and was followed by the generator powering down, and Jack beginning to laugh.

Cora opened her eyes.

Alexis was sitting up on the autopsy table, delicately peeling electrodes from her temples. Her skin was pinker, with less of a gray undertone. The jumper cables holding the bundled wire in place were still clamped to her ankles and the left side of her collarbone, their sharp metal teeth indenting her flesh. Jack reached up and removed the first of them.

"How are you?" she asked. "Any disorientation? Any discomfort?"

"No," said Alexis. Her voice was low and sweet and lovely, without a hint of pain. She smiled at Jack, warm and utterly guileless, before turning her attention to the rest of the room. "It's so nice to meet you, all of you. Jack's told me so much about you."

"Alexis has died twice, and second resurrections are rarely without complications," said Jack, removing the second clamp. "She needs regular infusions of lightning to remain stable, and there wasn't time to charge her up before we fled. Dr. Bleak gave everything he had to buy us the time to escape. Honoring his sacrifice"—her voice cracked—"was the least we could do."

"What *happened*?" Kade asked.

Jack took a deep breath. "I suppose I owe you the truth," she said. "After all, I've come to ask for your help. But I warn you, this isn't a tale for the faint of heart. It is a story of murder, and betrayal, and sisterly love turned sour."

"So it's a Tuesday," said Sumi. "We can take it."

Jack nodded. "As you say. It was, as it so often is, a dark and stormy night . . ."

4 A DARK AND STORMY NIGHT

"DR. BLEAK ALWAYS knew I'd return to the Moors eventually: the only question was whether I'd bring Jill with me." Jack leaned against Alexis as she spoke, like she was drawing strength from the other girl. "Some of the children who wander through our doors are clearly visitors, you see, while others are citizens who had the dire misfortune to be born into the wrong world. I was of the latter type. My sister's destiny was less obvious. When I opened the door home and carried her through, my teacher was waiting."

She closed her eyes, like she was struggling to put the moment into words.

Finally, sounding her age for the first time, she said, "He wept. My teacher, my . . . I hesitate to use the word 'master,' because that's what the vampire lord of our protectorate likes to be called, but still, my master, *wept*. He was so happy to see me that he lost his composure. He was so sorry to see my sister that he lost it even more. And then Alexis came out of the windmill, and I . . ."

She stopped. Alexis settled a hand on her shoulder, looking at the rest of them.

"I was dead when Jack and Jill fled the Moors," said Alexis, matter-of-factly. "Jill killed me, and Dr. Bleak wasn't certain the resurrection would take. Second resurrections don't, always, and my first death was how Jack and I met. She was Dr. Bleak's assistant for that revival. She did an excellent job."

"Stop," said Jack, a faint blush rising in her cheeks.

"No," said Alexis, and kissed her temple.

The pause had been enough to let Jack regain her composure. She opened her eyes and cleared her throat. "I hadn't dared to even hope that Alexis would be alive when I came home. There were complications, of course—there are always complications—but she was alive, and I was in the Moors, and Jill could never become a vampire, because once a body dies, it forgets how to become immortal. We brought her back that same night, the three of us working together beneath the biggest, most glorious thunderstorm I'd ever seen, and it was paradise, it was everything the Moon could possibly have promised me, and it was *mine*. It was my happily ever after."

"'Ever after' only ever comes at the end of the story, and your story isn't over," said Sumi. "What happened?"

It was such a small question. It shouldn't have invoked

such a large response. Jack laughed, a choked, mirthless sound that matched the tears in her eyes and the tremble in her black-gloved hands. She reached up like she was going to adjust her bowtie, and stopped when her fingers found only skin of her throat and the lacy edges of her peignoir.

"My sister has dreadful taste in clothing," she murmured. "It's a form of bravado and a sort of bragging at the same time. 'Look at me, I'm so precious to the vampire lord, and he's so very, very rich, that I can swan about a world filled with mudholes and monsters and not worry about staining my pretty pastel dresses or being supper for something made entirely of terrible teeth.' It's appalling."

"Focus," said Kade.

Jack sniffed. "I'd like to see you crammed into a body that isn't yours, and see how focused *you* feel."

Kade raised an eyebrow.

"That isn't what I meant and you know it," snapped Jack. She took a deep breath. "I'm sorry. That was unkind of me. I . . . No, it wasn't happily ever after, however much it felt like it at the time. It was merely a pause before the storm. The Master heard of our return, you see, and we'd been gone for long enough that the village had forgotten my sister's transgressions. It doesn't pay to have a long memory in the Moors. There's always another monster sniffing at the gates, and dwelling on the ones that have already gone elsewhere can distract from the one at your door. Jill drew the first breath of her second life at midnight. The Master was on our doorstep before the storm could fade, demanding his daughter's return."

Jack paused. Then, in a soft, shamed voice, she said, "We gave her to him. We could have fought, I suppose—I *should* have fought; she's my sister, after all—but we'd just performed a resurrection, and I was wounded, and the Master is a powerful foe. It's unwise to anger him. Dr. Bleak left the choice to me, left it in my hands whether we returned my sister to her vampiric father figure or closed the doors against him and kept her by our sides. She was crying for him, straining against the straps holding her down, and I . . . I let her go. She wanted him so badly. He was *her* happy ending, and I suppose I thought . . . I thought . . . I thought if I could have my windmill, and my mentor, and my love, she should have *something*. She could never be a vampire. The murder she'd been banished for had been undone. Let her have what remained of her own story, and leave us in peace."

"The murders she did here weren't undone," said Christopher.

"Except mine," said Sumi.

"Still weird," muttered Cora. "But apparently, I'm the only one who thinks so. Apparently, the rest of you go around raising the dead when you don't have anything better to do. It's a miracle we have any graveyards left."

"Are you done?" asked Kade.

"Maybe," said Cora.

"Good." He turned back to Jack. "Please. Continue."

"There isn't much left to say," said Jack. "Jill returned home with her 'father.' I remained with Dr. Bleak and Alexis, in a windmill large enough to touch the sky, and I said 'this is enough, this is everything I've ever wanted.' And I . . . I was right. I was home, and happy, and for the first time in my life, some of the things that plagued me receded. I went into the garden without my gloves. Not every time, or when it had been raining—mud is still beyond me—but I picked tomatoes and got berry juice on my fingers and I didn't care, because Alexis was there, Alexis loved me, Alexis didn't blame me for what my sister had done. I helped Dr. Bleak refine the lightning treatments that kept her with us. I went into the village, to a bookstore that sometimes gets volumes from other worlds, and bought books on sign language, so we could talk when her voice failed her. Dr. Bleak and I began discussing what would happen when my apprenticeship ended. It was . . ."

She stopped. Finally, she sighed.

"We were children when we found our doors, all of us. Maybe they don't prey on adults, or maybe adults don't come back, but I've never met anyone who was considered fully grown by their original society before they found their first door. We were children when the worlds we'd chosen threw us back to the world where we'd been born, and we were children when we came here. Lost, frightened children clinging to the only rope we had, the only lifeline that would keep us from tumbling into the abyss of self-doubt and despair. In that windmill, with Dr. Bleak and Alexis, with the Moon watching over me, I started to feel like I could be an adult. Like I could be *happy* growing up and settling down, like I knew where I belonged. Perhaps I didn't watch Jill as closely as I could have. Perhaps there were signs I missed, signs that something dangerous and cruel was gathering at the edges of my little world. I was happy. That was my crime."

"If it was a crime, we all shared it," said Alexis. "None of us saw this coming. None of us had a clue."

"I am a genius, and should have known when the wolves were at my door, but thank you," said Jack. "You are, and will always be, more than I deserve."

"Stop flattering me and finish asking these nice people for help," said Alexis.

"Even so," said Jack. She looked at Kade. "Last night, as the sun was setting, the Master's forces attacked our windmill. They seized me. And they offered Dr. Bleak a choice. Perform a very specific procedure on my sister and myself, or see me ripped to pieces, and each piece thrown to a different corner of our world, to guarantee no resurrection would be possible. I was screaming, begging him to let me die, when they began threatening Alexis. I understood what they'd do to me, you see, and I was afraid—but not so afraid that I could countenance letting them harm my heart. Second resurrections always come with consequences. Third . . . if you're fortunate, or unfortunate, they can be done. They're never worth it."

"What did they do?" asked Kade.

"In this world, lightning is limited," said Jack. "It can strike down trees, turn sand to glass, provide the power that runs an engine, but it can't move the stars or raise the dead. In the Moors, lightning is the motive force that drives all things. When the heavens speak, the dirt obeys. With the right hands to guide the conversation, lightning can do anything. Dr. Bleak experimented with the exchange of minds when he was a young man. He wanted to be able to make things better for people, you see, to put them where they'd be happiest. If a young woman wants to run away to sea, and her brother wants to marry his sister's handsome swain, and all parties agree, why not oblige them?"

"I can think of about a hundred reasons, but please, continue," said Kade.

Jack rolled her eyes. "Stop limiting yourself to the possibilities of *this* world, and consider the possibilities of a better one. If someone's greatest talent is running, and their greatest dream is never needing to run again, why not make a willing exchange with someone who dreams of nothing but the road? The key word being 'willing.' Dr. Bleak quickly found that most people are quite attached to their bodies, and have little interest in selling them on a permanent basis, while the unscrupulous were readily prepared to kidnap and replace those whose bodies might purchase passage into the higher echelons of society. He shelved his experiments and moved on to more wholesome pastimes, most concerning the reanimation of the dead and the acquisition of chocolate biscuits."

"What," said Sumi.

"Chocolate biscuits are important," said Jack. "But we stray from the point. The Master's people demanded Dr. Bleak's cooperation. They demanded my consent. They had Alexis, and I was not in my right mind, and I agreed, because nothing could be worth losing her again. And the Master . . ." She stopped for a moment, gaze going distant.

Finally, voice low, she said, "The Master came, Jill by his side in her ribbons and lace, like she was a bride on her way to the perfect wedding night. He helped her onto the table and strapped her down, he kissed her forehead and told her he loved her, and when he turned his attention on me, every drop of blood in my body ran cold. He looked at me like he'd won. Like he'd finally, permanently, won. Dr. Bleak and Alexis had to lift me onto the other table. I was shaking so hard I couldn't move. I screamed for Jill to say she didn't want this, to tell her father she wouldn't do this to me, and she closed her eyes and smiled, and said . . ."

Jack stopped again, longer this time, before she was able to whisper, "She said I was only getting what I deserved, for trying to take eternity away from her. Even then, she couldn't understand why she couldn't have everything she wanted. There are *rules*. I tried to tell her, I did, and her Master told her not to listen, and she didn't. Dr. Bleak threw the switch. He didn't have a choice. There was no way left for us to win. And then the lightning—it had always been my friend before, it had always done what I asked of it, until I suppose I'd started to think of it as . . . as a tame thing, like a hound that knows its master. But it wasn't tame at all. It bit me, it bit me over and over again, with terrible teeth made of nothing but light, and I was screaming, and I could feel the tethers that held me to my body breaking, until the room looked wrong, fuzzy and out of focus and *wrong*, and the eyes I was looking through weren't mine, and I . . . I . . ."

Jack—calm, implacable Jack, the mad scientist who had stabbed her own sister rather than allow her to achieve her murderous goals, who had rarely been seen to be less than perfectly composed, dignified and serene—put her hands over her face and sobbed. Alexis put her arm around the slimmer girl's shoulders and looked gravely at the assembled students.

"Jack can't stay in her sister's body," she said. "It will break her. Maybe worse, it will destroy the Moors."

Cora frowned. "She just said she went willingly. Why can't she stay? If they're twins, it should be pretty much the same as being in her own body. Right?"

"Jack has OCD," said Kade. "She may never have seen a doctor to get a proper diagnosis, but she did her time with Lundy—you never knew Lundy; she died before you came back from the Trenches—and they figured it out. She can't stand being dirty. She can't stand things being out of place. Right now, for her, *everything* is out of place."

"Before she passed out for the first time, she said it was like there were spiders under her skin, crawling all over everything," said Alexis. "This can't go on."

"I guess I can understand why this is bad for *Jack*, but why is it bad for the Moors?" asked Christopher.

Sumi gave him a brief, pitying look before switching her attention to Alexis, and asking, "Did they kill Dr. Bleak before or after you ran?"

"He bought us the time to get away," said Alexis. "He wasn't dead yet when we fled the windmill. The Master was taking his time, you see, and I think he appreciated the cruelty of letting Jill use Jack's body to take Jack's mentor apart. They were going to hunt us down next, and make sure Jill could never be returned to her own form."

"Why?" asked Cora.

"Jack has never died," said Alexis. "Jack's body has never stopped breathing, never known the resurrecting kiss of the storm."

"Which means *her* body can still become a vampire," said Kade, dawning horror in his voice.

"Exactly." Alexis stroked Jack's hair with one hand. "The Master plans to make Jill his daughter in truth under the next full moon. He's convinced her that they can be vampire lord and vampire child together for all time. Only now the windmill stands empty, with no scientist to hold back the dark and no apprentice to risk the storm. This isn't how things are supposed to happen in the Moors. You can't have a single unopposed force. The Master will throw everything out of balance, and the wolves in the wood and the Drowned Gods in the sea and all the other monsters will rise up to set things right. People will die. Innocent people, whose only crime was being born in the path of titans. Please. You have to help us save our home. And while she's too damn stubborn to ask on her own behalf, you have to help *me* save Jack."

Silence fell, broken only by the soft, monotonous sound of Jack's sobs.

Kade was the first to speak.

"All right," he said. "If you've got a way to get us there, I guess I better go talk to my aunt."

5 ANOTHER AWKWARD CONVERSATION

ELEANOR STARED AT Alexis like she was the most beautiful creature in the world, grayish skin and twisting scars and all. Alexis squirmed, not quite meeting Eleanor's eyes.

"*Look* at you," said Eleanor, for the third time. Her hands fluttered in her lap as if she wanted to reach for Alexis, only to think better of it at the last second. "I've never seen someone who was born in the Moors before, only children like dear Jack and precious Jill, who'd traveled there long enough to pick up a bit of local flair. You're lovely."

"Thank you, ma'am," said Alexis, voice turning hollow at the end of the sentence. She looked alarmed and glanced to Sumi, moving one hand in a quick, declarative motion.

"Alexis can't always talk," said Sumi. "She's died too many times. It broke something inside her, and now everything she does uses up a little of the lightning in her lungs, and when it runs all the way out, she has to be dead again until someone puts it back. She can sign, though. So I'm going to watch what she says, and then I'm going to say it to you."

"No embellishments, Sumi?" Eleanor managed to make the question sharp and gentle at the same time, like she already knew the answer but was willing to be kind about it.

Sumi narrowed her eyes. "I can embellish when I'm echoing somebody who doesn't need me to communicate for them, that's fine, that's fun, they can catch me out and call me a liar and we'll all laugh and laugh and laugh. Putting words in someone's hands when there's no one else around to tell you what they meant to say, that's not fair. I don't want to do that."

"All right, all right, I didn't mean anything by it."

Sumi's eyes remained narrow. "People always mean *something*. Sometimes what they mean is 'you can't be trusted to remember to be kind,' and then I want to bury them up to the necks in marshmallow fluff, so they'll remember how I choose kindness every single day."

Alexis looked wearily amused. Her hands moved. Sumi scowled.

"I am *not* like Jack, you take that back right now," she said.

Alexis shook her head.

Kade cleared his throat. "Sumi's promised to repeat what Alexis says fairly and accurately, and begging your pardon, ma'am, but I got the feeling we don't have a lot of time to waste deciding what we're going to do about the situation. Jill has Jack's body, and she's set on becoming a vampire while she's still wearing it."

"And if that happens, even if we catch her, we can't switch them back. Jack wouldn't like being a vampire," said Sumi. "Living on human blood, when it's all messy and dirty and filled with disease—no, she wouldn't like it at all."

Kade's lips thinned to a hard line, and he said nothing. He knew Jack well enough to suspect she might like being a vampire a little *too* much, maybe even more than Jill would. As a vampire, Jack wouldn't need to worry about getting sick, or be afraid she'd touch the wrong thing and somehow dirty herself beyond repair. She'd never been big on sunlit strolls or fancy dinners. Vampirism might suit her very, very well. An analytically minded vampire, fully trained to the inexplicable sciences of the Moors . . .

The people who fell in her shadow would find, quickly, that they'd have preferred the old-fashioned kind of vampire. In some ways, opera gloves and lacy peignoirs were less terrible than scalpels and tubing and spotless operating theaters. At least the first felt somewhat personal.

"All right," said Eleanor. She focused on Alexis. "You and Jack are both welcome here, for as long as you'd care to stay. I can arrange a room, board, everything, only let me know what you need."

Alexis's hands flashed.

"'It's kind of you to offer, but we can't stay,'" said Sumi. Her voice was calm, uncharacteristically level; in it, Kade could hear the echo of the girl she'd been before Confection, the one he'd seen in her permanent file, the one whose life had been measured and metered and entirely mapped out for her. She would have been a devastating woman, that solemn, mannered, well-educated daughter of privilege and plenty: she would have ruled a corporate empire with an unyielding fist, and her rivals would have trembled at her name.

That future had been sidelined when young Sumi found a door that wasn't supposed to exist; that version of her would never come to pass. Kade watched her translating for Alexis, and couldn't help but be oddly grateful.

Alexis continued to sign: Sumi continued to speak. "'The longer Jill has possession of Jack's body, the harder it'll be to take it back. More importantly, it will also be harder for Jack to adjust. Every minute is another minute when Jill could be touching anything with Jack's unprotected hands, wading barefoot in mud just because she knows it would cause her sister emotional distress—even killing people. Jack is more delicate than anyone knows she is. Jill is the only person she's ever killed, and she did it both to save her friends and with the full knowledge that Jill could and would be resurrected.'"

"Couldn't Jack learn to be happy in the body she has?"

asked Eleanor. "They're identical, or they were, before their choices caused them to diverge. Jack could make those choices again. She could make herself over in her own image, without needing to put herself in danger."

Alexis started to sign. Sumi shook her head, and she stopped, as Sumi rounded on Eleanor.

"No," she said. The calm was gone from her voice, replaced by all her hero's wildness, which cut through the whimsy she draped around herself like a knife through taffy. "No, and no, and *no*. You're better than those words, Ely-Eleanor, you're better than those *thoughts*. No one should have to sit and suffer and pretend to be someone they're not because it's easier, or because no one wants to help them fix it. Jack isn't Jill, and Jill isn't Jack, and if Jack wants her own body back, we're going to help her get it. You don't have to give us your permission. We can just go."

"They won't be going alone," said Kade. He looked at Eleanor, who he loved so dearly, and saw the echoes of his mother in her face, tucked into the wrinkles at the corners of her eyes and around her mouth. His mother loved him. He'd never been able to convince himself otherwise, even when it would have been so much easier to believe she didn't. But she couldn't—wouldn't—understand why he needed her to accept him as her son, when she'd loved him so completely as her daughter. "I'll be with them. So will Christopher and Cora, I reckon. Friends don't let friends go into danger alone."

"Oh, my sweet boy," sighed Eleanor. "I should have reminded you of the rules when Rini fell out of the sky. No quests. It's so easy to become addicted to them, and so hard to break the habit once it takes hold. What if you get hurt? What if the door back won't open for you?"

"Then we learn to live in the Moors," he said. "Christopher will fit right in. Everyone there probably thinks skeletons are charming. Alexis mentioned the Drowned Gods earlier, so I suppose Cora will have an ocean to get acquainted with, and as for me, I won't be any further from what feels like home than I am right now. We'll be fine."

"As long as there's butter, sugar, and flour, I know Confection will find me one day," said Sumi serenely. "I have to go home and get married in order for Rini to be born, remember? So it doesn't matter where I am. The door will find me."

"I don't think that's quite how it—" Kade began.

"Hey! Don't you go getting logical rules on my illogical life plans," said Sumi, cutting him off. "We're going. We're going to help Jack, and we're going to get the windmill back, whatever that means, so she and Alexis can do happily ever after forever and for always, not just until the vampires next door get bored."

"If you already knew you were going to go, why did you come to me?" asked Eleanor, in a voice that had grown very small.

"Because we love you, Eleanor-Ely," said Sumi. "We

didn't want you to just turn around and find us all gone away. That would be cruel. I can be a lot of things, and some are good and some are bad, but I try not to be cruel when I don't have to."

Eleanor took a deep, shuddering breath. She turned to Alexis and said, in a perfectly polite tone, "Anything you need, Kade can help you find. He's a good boy. He'll set you right."

Then she stood, reaching for her walking stick.

"I'm quite tired," she said. "I think I'm going to go and have a nap. Please be as safe as you can, children; please do your best to come home to me."

She turned, walking out of her own office, leaning on the stick a little more heavily than she had the day before. The door shut behind her. Alexis made an interrogative motion with her hands.

"The world gets heavy sometimes," said Sumi sadly. "That's all. She's carrying it as best she can, but . . . the world gets heavy. I hope she'll be able to put it down soon."

"Everyone puts it down sooner or later," said Kade. "The others should be ready for us by now."

Alexis signed something. Sumi nodded.

"As soon as we get back to the others, we're out of here," she said agreeably. "I've never traveled by lightning before. This is going to be fun!"

She skipped out of the room. Alexis and Kade exchanged a look.

"Not the word I would have chosen," said Kade. "Let's go."

Kade turned the office light off behind him, closing the door with a gentle click. It seemed like the least he could do.

6 LIKE LIGHTNING, BRIDGING THE SKY

JACK ADJUSTED HER cravat for the fifth time, considering her reflection. So much of what she saw in the mirror was simply, softly *wrong*, and virtually none of the people around her—people who, for the most part, thought they knew her, thought they were somehow equipped to understand her situation and the accompanying distress—could see it.

Oh, Alexis could, she was certain: Alexis knew every inch of her, even the ones she couldn't see, like the small of her back and the nape of her neck. Alexis had spent a satisfying amount of time with a compass and pen, drawing a careful chart of the moles and freckles that Jack's anatomy had conspired to conceal from her own eyes. With Alexis's help, Jack was solving the mystery of her physical form an inch at a time.

Freckles and moles. The bane of the fair-skinned, even when they lived in a place as gloriously clouded as

the Moors. *This* body no doubt had a completely different set of constellations scattered on its skin, as distinct as fingerprints, if far more potentially malignant. Jack shuddered at the thought, fingers slipping on the slick fabric of her cravat. Jill would never have thought to be concerned about something as simple as a spot, would never have realized she should worry about moles that grew too fast or changed color or shape. This body could already be dying, could—

"No," said Jack, loudly and clearly. Cora and Christopher, who were supposedly keeping her company but were really, she knew, standing guard, turned to look at her. She ignored them, focusing on the not-quite-right girl in the mirror. "That is a pointless spiral of fear and ignorance, and I refuse to let it claim me. Try harder."

Her mind—brilliant, traitorous, prone to devouring itself—did not stop fretting, but at least she was in control again. It was odd, to think of one's own mind as the enemy. It wasn't always. The tendency to obsession and irrational dread was matched by focus and attention to detail, both of which served her well in her work. She would have been a genius even without those little peccadillos. When she could keep her compulsions in check, make them *work* for her, she had the potential to be the greatest scientist the Moors had ever known.

But this body wasn't right, wasn't hers. The clothing Kade had so kindly fetched for her from his attic stronghold was only accentuating that reality, even after his

careful alterations. Her shirt was too loose in the arms
and shoulders, and even across the chest, although that
difference was less noticeable: Jill had never believed in
physical labor. Her trousers were too tight in the thighs
and buttocks—again, a slight difference, as Jill had always been troublingly focused on her weight, but still.
Every difference ached. Every difference *burned*.

Even her face was wrong. Different lines around the
mouth and eyes, from different uses of the underlying
musculature. People thought of Jack as the dour member
of the pair, and perhaps they weren't wrong, perhaps she
didn't smile as easily as her sister, but when she *did* smile,
she did so with sincerity. She smiled because she meant
it, a response that had already begun to translate into
specific morphology. Jill smiled because her Master liked
his daughter to be sweet and biddable, liked her to smile
in his presence as if he was the source of all that was
good in the world. Those smiles never reached her eyes.
Why should they? It wasn't like they were *real*.

"You all right over there, Jack?" called Christopher.

Jack swallowed a sigh. It would have been so much
better, so much easier, if she'd been the one to go and
speak with Eleanor. But if she had been forced to face
her former benefactor, if Eleanor had looked at her with
understanding—or worse, with *pity*—her narrow grasp
on her composure might well have snapped. She had
made excuses about becoming useless if she spent another
second in that lacy abomination Jill thought suitable for

an evening of body-snatching, claiming some indignities were simply too much to be borne.

The truth was simpler. She was reaching her limits. She couldn't stand to face one more person who understood how much she'd lost.

"No," she said, lowering her hands and turning to face them. "I'm so far from 'all right' that I doubt I could see it with a telescope. I never intended to come back here. This world is an affront to the scientific principles by which I live."

"You mean the scientific principles that let your sister steal your body?" asked Cora.

Jack frowned, focusing on the blue-haired girl. "Have I said or done something to offend you?" she asked. "Did I dissect one of your pets before I left here? That seems unlikely, since you joined the student body after my departure, but stranger things have happened. Time-traveling doors could be a real, if vexing, phenomenon."

Cora's ears burned red. "No," she said. "You just scared me with all that lightning. Someone could have been hurt."

"She means me," said Christopher. "I could have been hurt."

"Ah," said Jack. "I suppose pointing out that this was my room before it was Christopher's, and that the density of my belongings remains such that the principles of resonance still identify it as my domain won't buy me your forgiveness?"

"Since I have no idea what you just said, no," said Cora. "You can't go around electrocuting people. It's not safe."

"No one was hurt," said Christopher.

"I believe she's objecting to the possible, not the actual, which is something I can understand," said Jack. "I spend a great deal of my time contending with the possible, and sometimes must reject ideas I was deeply infatuated with because they have the potential to do more harm than I care for. I'm sorry I frightened you. It wasn't my intention. I won't say I would have done anything any differently, because I barely had time to calibrate the lightning rod before the fact that I was touching it with bare fingers—bare fingers that technically belonged to someone else—overwhelmed me, and I passed out from the shock. Our escape was a narrow thing. I would have been my sister's first meal in her new life had I remained where I was long enough to be taken, and so I can't apologize for fleeing. Only for the consequences it carried."

Cora paused, looking at Jack. She still didn't quite understand why identical twins trading bodies was so upsetting. That didn't change the fact that Jack *was* upset. Kade trusted her. Christopher trusted her. And Alexis trusted her, enough to stroke her hair and kiss her temples, even though Jack was currently in the body of the girl who had killed her.

"It's okay," she said. "I know you didn't mean it."

Jack inclined her head in acknowledgment. "Appreciated. Your hair—are you a Drowned Girl, like Nadya? Did you visit . . . I'm sorry, I can't pronounce it. The world with the Russian name and the fondness for turtles."

"Belyyreka, the Drowned World," said Cora. "No. I didn't go there. I went to the Trenches. I'm a mermaid."

"You're extremely bipedal, for a mermaid," said Jack.

"And Sumi is really talkative for a dead girl, but that doesn't shut her up," said Cora. "I'm a mermaid. I went into the water and I saw what I was always supposed to be, and I'm not giving that up because some stupid door decided I wasn't sure enough."

"Ah, surety," said Jack. "Have you noticed that the doors come for us when we're young enough to believe we know everything, and toss us out again as soon as we're old enough to have doubts? I can't decide whether it's an infinite kindness or an incredible cruelty." She looked at her hands, tugging the gloves more securely into place. "Perhaps it's both. Many things exist in a state of patient paradox, waiting for some change of circumstance to tilt them one way or the other."

"This is probably weird to say, given the circumstances, but I missed you," said Christopher.

Jack flashed him a quick, oddly shy smile. "Well, things must have been quite dull in my absence. I doubt any of these gutless churls would know how to de-flesh a body."

"No, that's not a common skill among the rest of the

current students," agreed Christopher. He glanced at the door before asking, "So . . . Alexis, huh?"

Jack's eyes narrowed. "Do you have an objection to my choice of partners?"

"Not at all! I mean, my true love is *literally* a skeleton, so I figure I don't get to judge. People love who they love. I just never thought you were into . . ." He paused, waving his hands as he tried to finish his thought.

"Fat girls?" asked Cora, a dangerous note in her voice.

Christopher snorted. "Please. Anyone with skin seems fat to me, including myself. Once you have working musculature, you're not my type."

"Disturbing but accurate," murmured Jack.

"I'm honestly more thrown by the 'person with a physical body' part," continued Christopher. "I guess I sort of assumed that one day you'd reproduce by budding, or by digging up a bunch of dead things and stapling them together."

"Alexis has been dead twice, and while she might be able to get pregnant via conventional means, neither science nor necromancy recommends she attempt to do so," said Jack. "I, on the other hand, am capable of reproduction when inhabiting my proper body, but find the idea abhorrent. It's a messy, dangerous process, and I want nothing to do with it. Should Alexis decide she wants to be a mother, I'll construct her the child or children of her dreams, and I won't use anything as primitive as a *stapler*."

"Why does that sound romantic when you say it?" asked Cora.

Christopher laughed. "Fair enough, biology bows before you. I got it. She seems nice."

"She's more than I, in all my weakness, could possibly deserve," said Jack. "She's the moon that lights my way and the stars that steer my course, and I spent every day I was enrolled in this school sharing a room with the sister who killed her, who'd never been able to understand what it was for me to be in love. When I arrived home and saw Alexis standing by Dr. Bleak's side, I felt . . ."

She stopped for a moment, throat working. Finally, in a soft voice, she said, "I felt like I'd been forgiven. I felt like I'd been rewarded for my willingness to stand against my sister, who I loved once—who I love still— with the restoration of the thing I cared for most in this or any other world. She's everything to me, and the Moors are her home, and I'll save them, for her. I won't pretend there's no selfishness here. I want my body back. Remaining in this one will surely drive me mad. But I'd accept that madness if not for the fact that Alexis would never forgive me for leaving her family behind."

Christopher whistled, long and low. "Invite me to the wedding, okay?"

Jack smiled. "I doubt you'll be able to handle the commute, but I'll light a candle to the Moon for you all the same."

The door at the top of the stairs banged open and Sumi came skipping down, pausing when she saw Jack. Then she lit up, bouncing onto her toes and grinning as widely as her face allowed. "*There* you are!" she declared, loud enough that people could probably hear her three rooms away. "I wondered, but you put your petals back in place, and you're the right rose after all! We're going to have an adventure, did you know?"

"Miss West agreed, then?" Jack looked past Sumi to where Kade and Alexis were descending the stairs. "You'll accompany us to the Moors?"

"We will," said Kade. "You're sure you can get us back here, right? This isn't a one-way trip?"

"Dr. Bleak will gladly reward you for assisting us, if he's able," said Jack. Her face twisted, sorrow and resignation warring for ownership of her expression. "And if all is as I fear it may be, I'll stand in his stead as new scientist to the Moors, heir to all the Moon's commands. Either way, the lightning will see you home."

"Jack . . ." Kade hesitated. "That sounds like a pretty permanent position."

"The first marriage any scientist makes is to their art," said Jack. "The second, if they're fortunate, is to someone somewhat softer. I've found both the loves of my life, and I'm not so arrogant—although I am, let us be clear, *quite* arrogant—as to think I could do better. I'm going home. I'm taking up the place I have trained for since I was a child, if that's what has to happen. Or perhaps I'm getting lucky, and Dr. Bleak will rise and hold his title for a little longer."

The look in her eyes made it clear that she didn't expect any further luck to be coming her way. She turned to Christopher and Cora.

"You're quite welcome to accompany us: Christopher, at least, has skills that would serve him well in the Moors, and I'm sure you"—she nodded to Cora—"have useful things to offer, although I don't know you well enough to guess at what they might be. The choice is yours. I should warn you that there are shadows in the sea where I come from. They might be more interested in you than you'll entirely care for."

"What, having managed to nab Kade and Sumi, you're happy to leave the rest of us behind?" asked Christopher.

"Having managed to 'nab' the Goblin Prince in Waiting and the war heroine, you mean? Yes, I'm quite content. But we're wasting time. Will you come, or no?"

"We'll come," said Cora, before Christopher could speak. She knew what his answer was going to be, could see it in the way he held his flute. He was hungry for adventure. He wanted to glut himself on it, to digest it slowly through the days ahead. Whether his door came for him again or not, he could at least remember there was magic in the world.

She didn't think she could bear it if he left her behind.

Jack nodded, relief flickering across her face like lightning licking at the sky. "I swear I'll do my best to get you home. Alexis?" She turned to the larger girl. "Will you do the honors?"

Alexis reached into the pocket of her apron and pulled out a key. Or at least, Cora *thought* it was a key; it didn't seem like it could be anything else, given the way it fit into the curve of Alexis's fingers. She'd just never seen a key crafted from living lightning before. It bucked and struggled against Alexis's grasp, trying to break free and ground itself.

Alexis stepped forward and slid the key into the empty air, closing her eyes. Jack put her hands over Alexis's, stepping closer, so the two girls were pressed together, holding each another steady, holding each other up.

"We're sure," said Jack, and together, they turned the key.

The room flashed white with lightning. It poured from the light fixture, cascading over Jack and Alexis before slamming, again and again, into the already-blackened floor. Alexis's unbound hair stood on end. Jack's hair, confined by a tidy braid, was more restrained, but Cora realized she could hear something under the pounding of the lightning.

Laughter.

Jack was laughing, high and bright and utterly delighted. It was the laughter of a child waking on Christmas morning to find a pony tethered to the bannister;

it was the laughter of a monster rising from the primordial ooze to devour the world. Cora wasn't sure which of those two thoughts frightened her more, and it was almost a relief that the lightning already had the hairs on her arms and the back of her neck standing on end, so she didn't have to blame it on the laughter.

Thunder rolled through the room, loud enough to vibrate the shelves, and the lightning stopped. The key remained, now protruding from the brass keyhole of an old oak door. Jack grasped the handle.

"All right," she said. "Let's go home."

PART II

THE MOORS

7 THE ROLES WE CHOOSE OURSELVES

THE OAK DOOR opened on a rolling hillside that stretched on for the better part of forever. Crimson moonlight painted every curve and corner, draping it like a shroud. Knee-high grass covered the landscape, peppered with patches of flowers, thorn brakes, and stunted, twisting trees.

Alexis was the first through the door, followed by Sumi, then Kade, Christopher, and Cora, with Jack bringing up the rear. For a moment the door remained open, showing a narrow slice of Christopher's basement bedroom. Then it swung closed, vanishing in the same instant, so that there was nothing but the Moors.

None of them noticed. Jack was too busy closing her eyes and breathing deeply; Alexis was too busy tucking the lightning key back into her apron. As for the others, they'd never been to this particular world before, and they were too busy staring.

Ahead of them lay the sea, great and roiling and terrible; something about it called to Cora and repulsed her at the same time, cautioning her that these depths would hold things she'd never seen in the Trenches, things that might not be as friendly as the monsters she'd already faced and defeated. Behind them loomed the mountains, craggy peaks covered in snow and dotted with castles. Kade knew without asking that there would be goblins, of a sort, in those high reaches, and that they would know him if he went to them, if he bowed his head and asked to see their king.

To the right stretched open fields, heading toward some distant village, some unknown monster. And to the left there stood a windmill, and beyond that in the far distance, a village splashed across the hills like it had fallen from some great and unknowable height, watched over by the towering, somehow terrible shape of a castle which seemed to defy all laws of architecture and good taste at the same time. It was a monster in its own right, and when it opened its mouth to feed, it would devour the world.

Sumi looked up and smiled serenely. "Look at the moon," she said. "It's like the sugared cherry on the biggest murder sundae in the whole world."

"Not a bad description," said Jack. "The Moon and the Moors are connected; She watches over us, and while She might not always approve, She remembers all."

"That sounds almost like superstition; Jack, I didn't

know you had it in you," said Kade, teasing to cover his own nervousness.

Jack looked at him blandly. "It's not superstition when it's a proven scientific fact. The rules are different here. Remember that, and you'll be fine. Now we need to hurry."

"I thought you said we had until the next full moon," said Cora.

"We do, but the Moon waxes and wanes more quickly here than she does in the world we were all born to: the last full moon was six days ago, and the next will come three days from now. At the moment, however, that is less important than the fact that sunset is approaching, and no one with any sense wants to be caught outside when the sun goes down."

Christopher blinked slowly. "You mean it isn't night already?" The world was overcast and gray, and together with the nearness of the bloody moon, it seemed reasonable to assume they were walking washed in moonlight, with no reason for the sun to get involved.

"Night is a much deeper darkness," said Alexis. "We need to get to cover. The windmill will welcome us." Unspoken was the fact that, if Dr. Bleak still lived, they would find him there.

"Lead the way," said Kade.

Jack did exactly that, stepping across the uneven ground with the graceful ease of long practice. The others followed, some more easily than others. Sumi skipped, as carefree as if this were a trip to an amusement park built on questionable design choices. Cora took quick, careful steps, skirting the various gopher holes—which, she suspected, hadn't really been made by anything as friendly as actual *gophers*—and questionable vegetation. Christopher, on the other hand, managed to trip three times in the first minute and a half, causing Jack to look at him and mutter caustically about setting records.

The whole time, Cora could hear the singing of the sea. It was a soft, ceaseless sound, and it matched the timbre of her heartbeat, echoing through her entire body. Maybe they could go there, when they were done at the windmill.

Maybe she could touch the waves. *Maybe the waves could touch me,* she thought, and the idea was and wasn't hers at the same time, and it was as enthralling as it was horrific, and she kept on walking.

None of the others noticed the growing vacancy in her eyes. Maybe that was for the best; there wasn't much they could have done about it. Kade fell back until he was walking alongside Alexis. "Hey," he said, voice pitched low, in the hopes that it wouldn't carry to Jack. "We haven't had much of a chance to talk. I'm—"

"I know who you are," said Alexis, amused. "I know all of you, except for the girl with the ocean in her hair. You're the stories Jack tells me at night, when my scars ache and I can't get to sleep. You're the children of the doors. You share something with her that I never will, and I suppose I ought to resent you for that, but honestly, I'm just glad you were there for her when I couldn't be."

"Ah," said Kade. "I'm not sure how I feel about being someone else's bedtime story."

"Everyone is somebody's bedtime story," said Alexis. "Most of us just don't have to face it so directly. I thought you'd be taller."

"I wish I were taller."

Alexis smiled, a twinkle in her eye. "Don't say that where Jack can hear you. She likes any excuse to grab a shovel and get to work."

"I'll keep that in mind." Kade hesitated before saying, with as much delicacy as he could manage, "The lightning that summoned the door seems to have given you your voice back. Do you know how long that's going to last?"

"I have a reservoir filled with lightning under my heart," said Alexis. "How fast it runs down depends on a lot of things. My voice is usually the first thing to go, followed by my balance, followed by the strength in my arms and legs. Eventually, I wind up unable to move without hurting so much it feels like the storm that brought me back to life is ripping me to pieces. I don't know how long I could stay that way without dying. I've never felt like it was important to learn. Is that what you wanted to know? Would you like more details? I'd offer to show you my scars, but Jack might notice if I started pulling off my clothes, so I'd prefer not to."

Kade winced. "You're angry."

"A little bit, yes. I understand wanting to know what your allies are capable of, but the fact that I've been damaged doesn't make me broken, and you don't need to behave as if it does. This is my home, my world, and I'm going to fight to get it back, just as hard as Jack will. Harder, maybe. She'll always be a newcomer here. She loves her land, and she'll protect it, but this is where I was born. The Moon has known my first breath, all three times I've taken it, and She loves me all the same."

Kade nodded, and was silent.

Ahead of them, leading the ragged gang of teens across the impossible landscape, Jack suddenly stiffened. All of them could hear her anguished cry of "Dr. Bleak!" before she broke into a run, moving with surprising speed over the uneven ground.

Sumi raced after her, easily matching Jack's sudden, panic-driven speed. Christopher and Kade were close behind. Alexis didn't run. Alexis walked with quiet resignation, as if she knew that hurrying would change nothing.

She paused for a moment when she reached Cora, who had stopped dead in her tracks, and whose eyes were filled with iridescent swirls, like sunlight dancing on the surface of the sea. Alexis bit her lip.

"I don't suppose it would make any difference if I said that you're supposed to help us save the world, would it?" she asked.

Cora didn't move.

Alexis closed her eyes.

She should have anticipated this, should have found a way to warn Jack of the risks—but then, it was so unpredictable, who'd be called and who wouldn't be, when they tumbled through the doors. The Master had called the Wolcott girls to him through the sheer force of his wanting, plucking the twin foundlings out of their uncertainty when either one of them could have been his beloved little girl. Dr. Bleak had stolen Jack away, but only because Jill would never have been able to walk away from the Master alive. Christopher's heart was sworn to a girl with fingers of bone and butterflies where her heart belonged. Kade was . . . well, based on what Jack had said about him, Kade was sworn to the school.

This girl, though, this girl, with the ocean in her hair and the scales melting under her skin, she'd been vulnerable from the start.

Alexis opened her eyes in time to watch Cora turn away from the windmill, toward the ancient, swallowing sea, and break into a run. She moved faster than seemed possible, legs devouring distance the way a storm devoured ships. In a moment, she'd be gone.

Alexis whirled and ran, not after Cora, but after the others. She caught up with Kade first, grabbing him by the arm and yanking him to a halt. He turned to stare at her, startled and a little angry, only to pale when he realized Cora wasn't with her.

"What—" he began.

"The Drowned Gods are singing a song that only your friend can hear," she said. "I'd never make it to the shore. Someone has to go with her."

Kade's expression faded into blankness. "The Drowned Gods," he repeated. "What the hell does *that* mean?"

"It means that sometimes, the Moors claim their own," said Alexis. "Please. She's getting away." She pointed toward the horizon, where a flicker of blue-green hair was still visible against the washed-out colors of the field.

Kade hadn't been as loud or as flashy in his heroism as Sumi, but he was still the Goblin Prince in Waiting; he had still saved his share of lives. He nodded, once.

"Tell Jack I'll find her," he said, and then he was gone, running after Cora, leaving Alexis standing alone in the middle of the Moors.

Slowly, the girl with the lightning-powered heart turned and trudged toward the windmill, and the inevitability of what she knew she'd find there.

8 EVERYONE HAS A MASK

SEEN UP CLOSE, the windmill was surprisingly pastoral. The walls were half-covered in trellises that dripped with bean runners and massive white flowers, their petals edged in lurid red. A low stone wall surrounded the gardens, and a cobblestone path led from the gate to the open door. The stones had been gray when they were pressed into place, each chosen for the precision of its fit with its neighbors.

The stones weren't gray anymore. They weren't red anymore, either. They were brown, the dark, rich, somehow carnal brown that comes only when blood is allowed to dry on some ordinary surface. The source of the blood wasn't immediately clear; it took a few seconds of staring after Jack for Christopher to realize that what he'd taken for an oddly shaped rock was actually a man's booted foot. He stopped running.

Jack didn't stop. Jack slammed the gate out of her way,

almost slipping on the cobblestones, and raced along the path until she reached the raised garden bed concealing the body attached to that foot. She dropped to her knees there, scrabbling for something the rest of them couldn't see, her face twisting into an expression of anguished disbelief. Then she began to wail.

Christopher winced. Jack had always been so self-assured, so mature; even when she'd first arrived at the school, she'd carried herself like she was much older than her actual years, like she was just waiting for the calendar to catch up with the woman she already knew herself to be. That girl was gone. In her place was a wailing, keening child, tears streaking her cheeks and snot running down her upper lip as she struggled to gather the hidden man's bulk in her arms.

Sumi trotted after Jack, not stopping until she was close enough to look down and see what Jack was clinging to so tightly, what she was trying so hard to pull into her arms. A flicker of sympathetic pain crossed her face, replaced almost instantly by her customary air of unconcern.

"Is it harder to resurrect someone who doesn't have a head?" she asked—and if she pitched her voice so it would carry to Christopher and warn him of the situation, Jack didn't seem to notice. "It seems like it would be harder."

Jack bent forward until she was folded nearly double, wails dwindling to an almost-inaudible weeping. Christopher took a deep breath and stepped through the gate, walking along the bloody path until he could see what was going on.

He immediately wished he hadn't.

Dr. Bleak's body was massive: it filled most of the space between two garden beds. He hadn't gone down without a fight: deep gashes marked his arms, and his chest looked like it had been sliced nearly in two. Most of the stump of his neck was hidden by Jack, who was kneeling where his head should have been, her folded arms resting on his chest as she sobbed into her hands. There was blood in her hair. For once in her life, she didn't seem to notice, or care.

Sumi circled the windmill, humming and picking ripe tomatoes from the garden beds. "I thought you needed sunlight to grow tomatoes," she commented idly. "You could sell a shade-growing variety for a whole lot of money, I bet."

"Sumi," hissed Christopher.

"What? The world doesn't stop spinning because you're sad, and that's good; if it did, people would go around breaking hearts like they were sheets of maple sugar, just to keep the world exactly where it is. They'd make it out like it was a good thing, a few crying children in exchange for a peace that never falters or fades." Her face hardened. "We can be sad and we can be hurt and we can even be killed, but the world keeps turning, and the things we're supposed to do keep needing to be done.

It's time to get up, Jacqueline Wolcott. It's time to remember what needs to be done for this cookie to crum-
ble the way you want it to."

Slowly, Jack lifted her head. Alexis had reached the
gate.

"The ocean caught your mermaid," she said, voice
soft and broken, like the wind whistling through the
eaves. The lightning in her heart was running out. "She's
gone to the Drowned Gods. The goblin went after her.
I'm sorry. I couldn't stop her."

Jack looked at her with an all-encompassing blankness in her eyes. "What?"

"The mermaid ran and the goblin followed," said
Alexis, before repeating, "I'm sorry."

"Ah." Jack closed her eyes for a moment as she stood,
running gloved, bloody hands over her hair. "Complications. Why must people be so *difficult*? We'll go to the
abbey. We'll get them back. And then I want Dr. Bleak's
head, and the time to bring him back, and my own body,
and for my sister to pay for what she's done."

"Sounds like you want a lot of things," said Sumi.
"Let's get started."

Jack looked at her. "Aren't you worried about your
friends?"

Sumi shrugged. "They're your friends, too, or Kade
is, anyway, and you don't sound worried."

"I'm too terrified for anything as simple as concern."

"Good enough for me," said Sumi. "You don't live

long enough to come back through the doors if you're not a hero. They're heroes, or they were. They'll remember themselves or they won't. If they do, they earn themselves a little closer to home. If they don't . . ."

She shrugged again.

Jack blinked, slowly. "Sometimes I can forget how terrifying you are," she said. She pulled off her soiled gloves and dropped them into the mud. "This body is too weak for any real lifting. Will those of you with more upper body strength than a dead rat please bring the body? We have a great deal of work to do."

She turned and walked inside without waiting to see whether they were going to listen. It was clear she already knew the answer—and equally clear that she needed a moment to settle her thoughts.

Christopher walked around to the—well, the head of the body, which felt like a terrible joke—and looked thoughtfully down at the breadth of it. "I can hoist him, but we're going to need to work together. Sumi, if you can get the feet and Alexis can take the middle, we can do this."

"Yeah," chirped Sumi.

"Of course," said Alexis, shaking off her silence. They moved into position, and together, they hoisted Dr. Bleak off the ground, carrying him toward the windmill like pallbearers in search of a funeral. Sumi's mouth was slick with juice and seeds from her stolen tomatoes. Christopher looked away, swallowing bile. Under the red light of the rising moon, she looked far too much like a vampire.

The interior of the windmill was like Jack's room at school writ large and gloriously unconstrained. Shelves lined the walls. Each was laden with tools, raw materials, and the instruments of scientific sorcery. Strange taxidermy and bundles of herbs dangled from the vaulted ceiling, which extended upward to a pair of skylights, each surrounded in turn by a complex system of weights and pulleys. A spiral staircase wound its way up the direct center of the structure, pausing periodically to put forth narrow, dangerous-looking catwalks. Those connected, in their turn, to doors set into the windmill walls. All the additional rooms must have been constructed around the exterior, since there was no room in the middle.

A pair of large metal tables occupied the bulk of the floorspace, positioned equidistant from all three of the fireplaces. Leather straps made it absolutely clear that the purpose of those tables was, perhaps, not always pleasant. Several complicated if archaic-looking machines had been rolled up close to them, their thick black cords winding back to a system of portable generators and one large crank, for the occasions when variable power was needed.

Jack stood next to the larger table, hands resting against the metal and nails digging at the surface of the table like she thought she could wound it. The smear of blood on her left cheek seemed almost innocuous, after that.

"Bring him to me," she said, voice very soft.

So they did. They carried the body of Jack's mentor, cool and stiff with rigor, over to her. They hoisted him onto the table and stepped back, waiting to see what Jack would do.

Jack reached for the leather straps. "Alexis, bring me the dialysis array. Christopher, help me secure him."

"Do they not say 'please' in mad science land?" asked Christopher, even as he did what she'd asked.

"Not as a rule." Jack shook her head, pulling the first strap across Dr. Bleak's massive chest. "When a scientist speaks, it behooves the ordinary soul to listen. We rarely speak without cause."

"I thought dialysis was a modern thing, not a mad science thing," said Sumi. "You're mixing your genres."

Jack glanced up. "I come from the same world you do," she said. "I didn't forget the medical wonders of my youth simply because I chose a world where lightning is the panacea and thunder is the very voice of God. I'm not the only one to have made the transition, either. Much of what our birth world can do, the Moors can do, simply in a more dramatic and often more permanent fashion. Dialysis will let me keep Dr. Bleak's blood oxygenated and prevent further tissue damage."

"You're not *keeping* anything," said Christopher uncomfortably. "His blood isn't oxygenated anymore. It's dead. He's dead."

"Must I be surrounded by fools and cowards at every

turn?" Jack glared. "I've told you before, here, science is always the question, and the answer is always and eternally 'yes.' I'll suction the blood from his veins, re-inflate them with saline, and replace his blood, fully oxygenated, before capping the stump of his neck and beginning circulation. Yes, he's dead. Many people have been dead. Two of the people in this room have been—"

"Three," said Sumi with apparent disinterest, munching a tomato as if it were an apple and looking thoughtfully at the stuffed infant plesiosaur dangling from the ceiling.

Jack stopped. "I'm sorry?"

"Three of the people in this room have been dead. You're wearing Jill like a Sunday gown, and she was dead before you brought her here and brought her back, so three." Sumi shrugged. "It's something we all have in common, except for Christopher, and he loves a dead girl, so I guess he has it too, just sideways."

"Yes." Jack's hands dug at the edge of the table again, a look of brief, intense nausea on her face. "Three. As you say. It changes nothing. I'll restore his circulation and preserve his tissues. Resurrection is easier when decay hasn't had too much time to set in. The healing process is long enough without adding necrosis to the list of complications."

Alexis returned from the far side of the windmill, pulling a large machine with one hand and a pair of joined cannisters with the other. "Ready," she said.

"Excellent." Jack turned to the others. "Your services

are not currently required. Upstairs on the third floor, you'll find a room with a brown door. That's storage. Dr. Bleak and I moved the wardrobe up there when I began requiring my own workspace here. I suggest you go up and find yourselves something to wear, to make you slightly less conspicuous when we head to the priory. A band of hired heroes is tedious but mundane. Adventurers come from nearby protectorates to march on the castle all the time. A band of heroes from another world, however—that's certain to draw attention."

Sumi calmly tipped her remaining tomatoes onto an open patch of counter and made for the stairs. Christopher followed her. She had a good instinct for when it was time to get out, and more, Jack was reaching for a tray of knives, scalpels, and what looked suspiciously like a bone saw. Making a quick exit seemed like the better part of valor.

The stairs were narrow but sturdy. Christopher saw something dangling from a rafter, and decided not to tell Sumi about the windmill's apparently sizeable bat population. It would just be one more complication, and they had plenty of those already.

He glanced down only once before following Sumi into the room Jack had indicated. She and Alexis were moving around the body of Dr. Bleak, tightening straps, inserting tubes, silent and comfortable in their work. He watched them for a moment. Then he turned, and stepped through the door, closing it firmly behind him.

The room was small, made smaller by the wardrobes and chests along the walls. They were made of sturdy cedar, and there was no dust, no cobwebs, even though both would have suited the overall aesthetic of the Moors. Christopher ran a finger over a piece of decorative molding, smiling when it came up clean.

"I guess having Jack as an apprentice is sort of like having a live-in housekeeper who sometimes gets pissed and throws stuff," he said.

Sumi cocked her head, considering him. "You're awfully hung up on the mundane things," she said. "Is this because you traveled through Logic, or are you afraid?"

"Aren't you?" asked Christopher.

"No." Sumi's smile was bright as the absent sun. "I don't die here. I make it back to Confection. One day I die there, and my body goes into the ground for the gummy worms to eat. But even if I did die here, I wouldn't be afraid. This is *new*. I've never fought a *vampire* before, or tried to steal someone's body back. New things are the best kind of magic there is. I can't waste time being afraid when there's newness to roll around in, like a dog in a puddle of syrup."

"That's a terrifying visual," said Christopher. He pulled a dress covered in virulently blue and orange stripes out of the wardrobe and made a face. "I thought horror movies were supposed to be all monochrome and serious. This hurts my eyes."

"It's perfect," said Sumi, snatching it out of his hands and peeling off her shirt.

Christopher looked up at the ceiling. "I wish you wouldn't do that."

"And I wish you weren't so weird about nudity, but here we are, and here we go, and you need to find something to wear," said Sumi. She had pulled the brightly colored dress on and was doing up the laces, expression approving. "This is so good. Think I can keep it when we're done? If I don't get too much blood on it?"

"Probably," said Christopher, poking around in the wardrobe for something in his size. "Do you think Jack's stable right now? Can we trust her to make good choices?"

"I don't think she's any more *un*stable than she was when she showed up in the basement," said Sumi. She shot Christopher a look. "Misfit toys forever, remember? She's one of us. She was there at the beginning. She'll be there at the end. We help her when we can."

"Her sister killed you."

"I got better," said Sumi airily.

Christopher laughed and pulled a white linen shirt out of the wardrobe. "Right," he said. "I forgot."

In the end, he was able to find trousers, a white linen shirt, and suspenders that fit him almost identically to his normal jeans and T-shirt. They felt like clothes, not a costume, something that he tried not to dwell on too much as he followed Sumi back out onto the stairs.

She gripped the rail and leaned out as far as gravity allowed, shouting, "We're properly dull now! Are you done playing with corpses?"

"Show some respect, you incomprehensible beast," Jack called back—but there was no rancor in her voice. If anything, she sounded relieved, like she'd been hoping for a distraction.

"No," said Sumi. "Do you think if I jumped from here, I'd break *both* my legs?"

"If you do, I'll build you new ones," said Jack.

Sumi laughed and went dancing down the stairs, Christopher following after. Jack and Alexis had draped a sheet across Dr. Bleak's body; if not for the unpleasant void where his head should have been, it would have been almost possible to pretend he was asleep. The void, and the tubes running from the body to the dialysis machine, which was clicking along, making strange grinding sounds that must have been perfectly normal, since neither Jack nor Alexis looked alarmed.

The tubes were filled with thick red fluid the consistency of raspberry jam, and much as Christopher wanted to tell himself that it wasn't blood, it was blood. His capacity for self-delusion had never been terribly high. If it had been, he might have been better at lying to his parents, and his life might have turned out very differently.

Jack had also taken the time to change her shirt, wipe the blood from her face, and put on a fresh pair of gloves. There was still a faintly disheveled air to her. It made

Christopher nervous. Jack wasn't supposed to be disheveled. Jack was supposed to be arrogant, immaculate, and utterly self-assured. She was falling apart more quickly than the rest of them realized—maybe more quickly than *she* realized. She was doing her best, though. That had to count for something.

It would, if they stood by her and made sure she got her happy ending. Whatever shape it took. "What do we do, Jack?" asked Christopher. "This is your world. Tell us what to do, and we'll do it."

"We can't march on the village at night; that would be suicide, and without Dr. Bleak to harness the lightning, none of us would come back from that, which means no one would be able to fetch Cora and Kade back from the Drowned Gods," said Jack. "I think Miss West would be quite cross if I got that many of her students killed."

"If you got *any* of her students killed," said Christopher. "Say it with me: Miss West would be pissed if you got *any* of her students killed."

Jack waved a hand dismissively. "Death is a temporary setback. We can go to the village at dawn. The Master's housekeeper, Mary, remembers me from when Jill and I first found our door. I believe she'll let us into the castle if I ask nicely, and if I promise that she won't be held responsible for the Master's actions, should our side win. For now, tonight, I have another destination in mind. We need backup, and we need to recover our friends before something dire happens to them."

"Define 'dire,'" said Christopher.

"The Moors are more complicated than they seem at first glance. We're in the Master's protectorate, where my status as Dr. Bleak's apprentice grants me a certain measure of protection. It's easy to dismiss the rest as the part of the map that reads 'here be monsters,' but that's not quite accurate. The werewolves hold the high mountains and the forested places; apart from the gargoyles and a few very ancient, very powerful vampires, no one challenges their dominion. They have too many teeth to be safely argued with. The heath is divided among a variety of lesser monsters, such as the Master and Dr. Bleak—and one day, if I keep to my studies, me." Jack smiled, quick and bright as a knife in the darkness. "Every monster has its natural counterbalance. Vampires and mad scientists are well-matched enough to keep the peace, even if it's sometimes kept in pieces."

Only Sumi laughed. Christopher and Alexis looked at her, and she shrugged. "What? For Jack, that was a very funny joke. We should give her a gold star for trying."

"As I was saying," said Jack. "Dr. Bleak is dead and I am his heir: technically, a challenge has begun. The other monsters of the flatland will be watching to see who comes out on top, and they won't interfere. If the Master kills me and turns Jill, an imbalance will be established, and those same monsters will come to correct it. I'm sure that will lend some small measure of comfort to my loved ones."

Alexis glared at her.

"So where are we going?" asked Christopher.

"To the seashore," said Jack. "The Drowned Gods have taken Cora. They've given us nothing in return. I want her back or, if they refuse, I want their help in setting things right."

"Now hold on," said Christopher. "Cora's not a bargaining chip. She's not going to stay with these 'Drowned Gods' of yours, no matter what they say."

"You misunderstand," said Jack. "The Drowned Gods are horrors beyond comprehension. We won't approach them directly. We'll be speaking with their High Priest, who can hopefully give aid to our cause—and return Cora to us unharmed."

"Unharmed, but not unscathed," said Sumi. Jack and Christopher turned to look at her. She shrugged. "I listen to what you're not saying. Water changes things."

"Yes," said Jack. "It does."

"Just so you know," said Sumi. "This sounds like a good way to not get anyone killed. Let's do it."

"Anyone else," said Jack.

"What?"

"We might be able to do this without getting *anyone else* killed," said Jack. "Dr. Bleak is dead. Even if we're able to undo it—and I can't guarantee we will be; he died at least once before I came to the Moors—he will still have been killed. He will still have died for the sake of giving me, and Alexis, the chance to get away. We don't get to ignore that."

"Alexis has died twice," said Christopher. "She's fine."

"I'm not, though," said Alexis. She twisted her apron in her hands. "I have lightning where my heart should be. If it goes away, my body stops functioning. I love Jack more than I ever thought it was possible to love another person, but it wouldn't matter if I stopped loving her, because I can never leave her. There's not another windmill within three days' ride. I wouldn't make it to another table, another lightning array, before I collapsed, helpless, food for whatever monster might come along. I can never safely bear my own children. I can never have my own home. I'll be in this windmill as long as I'm alive, and sometimes living hurts. So no, second resurrections aren't the easy things people want to pretend they are. Actions have consequences."

Jack looked at her gloved fingers. "As my lovely lady so clearly states, we can't count on bringing anyone back. It would be better if we could do this with a minimum of bloodshed."

"I'm sorry," whispered Christopher. "I didn't know."

"Of course you didn't. This isn't your world. These aren't the rules you learned to live by. We have certain advantages here that the world of my birth lacks—we have the lightning—but we must find a way to use them that serves us, and not the Master's terrible goals." She looked up again. "We'll approach the acolytes of the Drowned Gods and ask their aid. If they'll grant it to us, we may be able to end this."

"When?" asked Sumi. "Do we wait until morning?"

Jack shook her head. "We leave at once. Dr. Bleak's head lacks the scientific support I've given to his body. If he's to have any chance to rise again, we must act quickly."

"Wait," said Christopher. "You said no one with any sense would want to be caught outside when the sun went down."

"Yes, and now the sun *is* down, and the night creatures have stirred themselves to begin hunting. The danger of sunset is proximity to their dens and hidey-holes. They tend to be hungry when they wake, and no one ever sneered at a self-delivering meal." Jack took Alexis's hand. "Alexis will stay here to monitor Dr. Bleak's condition and keep the doors barred against intrusion. Jill isn't a vampire yet; the balance of power has yet to fully tip in the Master's favor. He won't come here again."

"This place is made of straw and stone and fizzy chemicals," said Sumi. "I don't understand why the Master didn't just light a match. Oopsie, there goes my rival, up in flame and fireworks. It would have been easier."

"Easier, certainly, but it would have betrayed the balance, and the balance is everything," said Jack. "If he'd burnt the building down around our ears, the other Masters, the other Doctors, they would have descended like all the demons of Hell itself coming for retribution. This is a challenge. The Master seeks complete dominion to hand to his newly minted daughter. That means he'll seek to take things quickly and cleanly, and without violating any of the traditional rules."

"Body-snatching is in the traditional rules?" asked Christopher.

Jack didn't roll her eyes . . . quite. Christopher realized that she was wearing different glasses now, the frames a little rougher, the lenses a little thicker. They hadn't been made by a modern optometrist. They'd been milled and crafted here, in this laboratory. "When Jill and I arrived in the Moors, Dr. Bleak convinced the Master to let me live by pointing out that I could be an endless supply of spare parts for my sister. Here, bodies are just another tool, to be stolen or traded as the people in power see fit. Burning down someone's lab before they've been properly vanquished, on the other hand, is *rude*. Now ready yourselves. We've quite a way to go before we'll see anything akin to safety."

She turned to Alexis, offering her hands. Alexis smiled and took them.

"I wish you didn't have to stay behind," said Jack.

"It's better this way," said Alexis. "I can hook myself up to the generators if I start fading, and if the windmill lights are on, the Master's likely to think you're holed up in here, trying to forge a new head for Dr. Bleak. Let me buy you time."

"If the Master returns, run."

"I promise," said Alexis. She leaned down, and Jack leaned in, and two of them kissed like they were alone in the room, like no one else were watching.

When Jack pulled away from Alexis and started for the windmill's rear door, Sumi skipped over to walk beside her.

"I always knew you were more sugar than you pretended to be," she said blithely. "No one can go through life entirely spice. It wouldn't taste very good."

"A person is not a piece of gingerbread," said Jack.

"Oh, you're so wrong about that," said Sumi.

Outside the door was a wagon, half-filled with straw. Jack selected a pitchfork from an array of farming tools, handing it brusquely to Sumi.

"Make yourself useful and fluff the hay," she said. "Rats sometimes bed down in it during the day, and I would prefer no one get bitten. They carry disease, you know. Horrible vermin. Christopher, with me."

"What are we doing?" he asked, even as he was moving to join her.

Jack smiled, terrible and thin. "We're getting the horses. I think you'll find them to your liking." She turned and walked away, heading for a low, boxy outbuilding behind the main windmill. Christopher, as she had clearly anticipated, followed.

"We didn't have horses when I arrived here," she said. "They were something of a journeyman project for me.

I built the first before my tenure at the school, and the second after my return, once I realized how easily Alexis tires. Between the two of them, we can pull a wagon, and that has made all the difference for her in terms of freedom."

"You really love her, don't you?" asked Christopher.

"More than science itself," Jack replied. "If she bade me to flee to the school and leave the Moors to rot in their own effluvia, I'd do it, so long as she agreed to come. I'd even do my best to learn how to live in this body, for all that I can barely resist the urge to flense its skin off with my fingernails in the vain hope that the tissues beneath would be cleaner. Fortunately, she loves me with equal fervor, and would never ask such a thing of me."

Jack unlatched the stable door, paused, and looked at Christopher. "These are my horses, and are very dear to me," she said. "Please do not scream." Then she pushed the door open and went in, leaving Christopher with no choice but to follow.

"Well, this is probably how I die," he said, in a philosophical tone, and stepped inside.

9 AND THEN THERE WERE HORSES

JACK PAUSED JUST inside to light a small oil lamp. It illuminated the front of the stable, showing bales of hay and a few ratty blankets. The whole place felt like a fire trap. Christopher didn't say anything. He had to assume Jack knew what she was doing, or this whole expedition would devolve into a nightmare.

It sort of already had. Indoor lightning storms, resurrected girls, and giant, bloody moons were terrifying enough without throwing in headless corpses, vampire lords, and something called a "Drowned God." Mariposa had never been anything like this.

"Hello, sweethearts," said Jack, voice high and sweet and nothing like it normally was. "Who wants to go for a little trip?"

"Is that how you're supposed to talk to horses?" asked Christopher. "I always thought that was how you talked to—oh my God."

"Yes, well, horse brains in decent condition are harder to come by than you would think. Dog brains are substantially easier." Jack stroked the velvety patchwork muzzle of the first horse, offering it a fond smile. "It made training somewhat complicated, but they're generally eager to please."

"Uh . . . huh," said Christopher.

There were two horses in the pen. "Horses" was really the only word that could apply to them: while some other words might have been accurate, they were also, to a one, insulting, and Christopher was fairly sure Jack wouldn't approve. The first horse, the one Jack was stroking, appeared to have started its existence as several horses. Several horses and possibly, going by the shape of its left haunch, some sort of cow. The pieces had been cunningly stitched together, and while there were thin ridges of scar tissue between them, they had all healed cleanly, leaving a single intact mare behind.

It was impossible to tell whether the second horse was a mare, a stallion, or something else entirely, as it had no skin. No flesh, either; it was a tall skeleton, bones joined by loops of silver wire and complicated hooks. Dim lights gleamed in its eye sockets. It nosed at Christopher's shoulder before snorting loudly. An impossible gust of hot air ruffled his hair.

"How . . . ?" he asked.

"Science, for Pony," said Jack, patting the patchwork horse's shoulder. "Necromancy, for Bones. I had to ride

all the way to the next village. It's held by an old ally of Dr. Bleak's, a woman who lives in constant conflict with a terrible monster of her own creation who haunts the nearby fens. Really, I prefer vampires. They're tidier. Still, Pony requires more maintenance. Bits of her fall off all the time, and I wind up spending the evening sewing them back on."

"You named your horse 'Pony.'" Christopher couldn't take his eyes off Bones. The skeletal horse was the most beautiful thing he'd seen in . . . in . . .

In a very long time.

"In my defense, I was *very* young, and had no sense of showmanship. Although I'll deny it if you tell anyone I said so, I'm glad I built her so early. 'Pony' is a much better name than 'Corpseblossom,' which is doubtless what she'd have been called if I'd put her together during my pretension and depressing poetry phase. Here." She tossed him a bridle. "See if Bones will let you put this on. We need to get them hitched and be on our way."

"Sure," said Christopher. He took the bridle and approached the bone horse, not warily, but reverently, like he couldn't believe his luck. "Aren't you beautiful? None of that messy skin to get in the way, oh, no, not for a horse as beautiful as *you* are . . ."

"See, this is why I like you," said Jack, quickly and expertly getting the bridle onto Pony. "You appreciate the finer things in life. Even Alexis had some issues with the fact that our new horse lacked skin. I tried pointing out that a lack of skin also meant a lack of hair, which meant substantially less shedding, but she remained unmoved."

"You're still weird." Christopher slipped the bridle onto Bones, smiling as the horse rubbed its naked skull against his hands. "I mean, cool, but weird."

"Aren't we all?" asked Jack, and opened the stall door.

Sumi, who had taken a seat atop the musty hay mounded in the wagon, cocked her head to the side.

"Christopher, when you look at that horse, does it have skin?" she asked. "If no, good. If yes, I probably shouldn't have eaten those tomatoes."

"My produce is not hallucinogenic," said Jack, leading Pony to the front of the wagon. "Christopher, hitch Bones over here and climb into the wagon with Sumi, if you'd be so kind. We can reach the shore by midnight, which should impress the acolytes. They do so adore punctuality."

"That horse doesn't have any skin," said Sumi. "And that other horse has too many skins. I think *one* is the traditional number of skins for a horse. Isn't it?"

"Good of you to notice." Jack climbed up onto the box seat, gathering the reins in her hand. Sumi scrambled over the board intended to support her back to join her. "Christopher, it appears you'll be riding in the rear."

"Shotgun," said Sumi unrepentantly.

"I don't mind." Christopher secured Bones, kissed the horse on the side of the skull, and walked around to hop up into the back. "As long as I can help you stable them later, I don't mind anything right now."

Jack flicked the reins and the horses plodded forward, slowly gathering speed, until they were moving at a brisk trot. The benefits of undead horses became quickly apparent: once the horses hit their stride, they neither slowed nor stumbled, but continued moving forward at a steady, measured pace. The wagon fairly flew across the uneven ground. There was no road, no path, only the scrub, and the holes left by the creatures that lived there.

The Moon seemed to have grown closer while they were inside the windmill. It loomed low and crimson and terrible, like a vast infected eye looking down from above. Sumi stared up at it like she was issuing a challenge, or maybe like she was answering one. If the Moon noticed, it gave no sign, and perhaps that was the greatest mercy the Moors had yet to show.

"This is a horror movie," she said, in a dreamy, thoughtful tone. "Did you know? We walked into a horror movie on purpose, and not everybody makes it out alive."

"Jill won't." Jack's voice was soft and implacable. She didn't take her eyes off the fields ahead of them. "I can't leave her alive, not if I want to have any confidence in waking up each morning in the shell of my own skin. She's the one who decided to escalate our conflicts into a war, not me. This isn't my fault."

"That sounds like a little bit of lying to yourself," said Sumi.

"It sounds like making certain I'll be able to sleep at night—something which is not, at present, guaranteed," said Jack. "Ah, well. The best scientists have grappled with insomnia."

"Couldn't you just . . . banish her?" asked Christopher. "The way Dr. Bleak did, when you both wound up at the school?"

"Banishment, of course," said Jack. "Remind me, how many people did she kill? How many more would she have slaughtered in her effort to reclaim what she thought was hers by right? I could send her back to the world of our birth, and when she carved a path through the bodies of its innocents, looking for a door to bring her home, would that blood be on her hands or my own? I have trouble enough staying clean. I would prefer not to make things worse."

Silence fell over the wagon, broken by the rattle of wheels against the ground, the hammering of hooves, and Pony—only Pony, not Bones—breathing. Finally, Sumi leaned over and patted Jack on the shoulder.

"Don't worry, we'll still love you after you kill your sister."

"How delightful for me," said Jack, and urged the horses on.

The smell of the sea reached the wagon moments before the sound of the water itself crashing against the unseen beach. It drowned out the thudding of the horses' hooves, growing louder with every passing second.

"A few ground rules, if you don't mind." Jack's voice was a razor, slicing across the crashing of the waves. "The villagers who live in the shadow of the Drowned Gods are pleasant folk, but they have strange appetites, and stranger ideas about hospitality. Accept nothing they offer. Assume that any pleasantry comes with attached strings, and ask yourself how many fingers you *need* before you return it in kind. They won't harm you if not given permission, but they may take simple courtesy as permission, and they are always, always hungry. Mind you"—amusement crept into her tone—"the one time a group of them came to meet with Dr. Bleak in the village, I heard their leader giving much the same warning about those who live in the shadow of a vampire lord, so it's entirely possible there's no strangeness here at all, merely a few small cultural differences and a great whopping dash of xenophobia."

"Don't you mean racism?" asked Christopher.

"'S'not the same thing," said Sumi.

"Much of the population of the Moors is made up of the descendants of travelers whose doors opened all over the world. In this case, I mean xenophobia," said Jack, voice surprisingly pleasant. "Were we attempting to parlay with the gargoyle kings, who detest and fear anyone not made at least partially of stone, I would mean racism. Regardless, I must ask you to be on your best behavior, at least until we reach the abbey. If you wish to offend *them*, do so with my blessing. I'll be standing at a safe remove, watching to see how far the entrails fly. Do we have an understanding, or must I provide details?"

"We understand," said Christopher hurriedly. "Please don't provide details."

"Excellent." Jack gave the reins a snap. The horses slowed. "We're here."

The others turned and beheld a wall that looked high enough to scrape against the omnipresent moon. It was made entirely of blackened timbers, barnacles and dried-out clams clinging to their sides, like they had been harvested from the greatest shipwreck the world had ever known. Slowly, the vast gates swung open, and with another flick of the reins, Jack drove them through, into the dubious safety of the town.

The gates slammed shut behind them with remarkable speed, and everything was quiet, and Christopher knew, with absolute certainty, that not all of them were going to make it home.

PART III

WHERE THE DROWNED GODS GO

10 WHERE THE SHADOW MEETS THE SEA

BUT WE MUST go backward, briefly: we must go back to a girl running, running, running across the vast sprawl of the Moors with her heart in her throat and her lungs achingly full of unfamiliar air. Air has never been her harbor, never been her home, and this air is less hers than most. This air burns. And still she keeps running, racing toward the shadow of the sea.

That's what called her, of course. The sea, the sea, the *sea*. A sea, not the strawberry soda of Confection, not the muddy turtle pond that kept her from drying out at school. She missed the depths so much some days that she couldn't concentrate on anything except how much she wanted to go home. The other students would talk longingly about endless skies and forests filled with talking flowers, but none of them understood, because they'd always been air-breathers. They'd gone from one world filled with wind and light and gravity to another, and they didn't know how much she'd lost.

In the Trenches, "up" and "down" had been a matter of consensus. Oh, the surface and the bottom existed, but they were inconsequential things. The people of the Trenches measured by depths and shallows, and they danced their way from one side of the ocean to the other. They breathed the living sea, and the sea rewarded them by keeping them as safe as she was able—which wasn't very, because the water was filled with countless dangers, and none of them mattered in the face of the absolute, indisputable fact that the water was *home*.

When Cora's door had tossed her unceremoniously back into the world of her birth, she hadn't only lost adventure. She'd lost weightlessness, freedom, *flight*. She'd lost her entire native environment. She ran, as caught as any fish snared by a fisherman's lure, and wondered distantly whether she was going to throw herself off the first cliff she saw, convinced all the way to the bottom of her bones that she'd transform as soon as she struck the sea.

She wondered whether it was going to hurt.

She wondered whether she was going to care.

Behind her—far behind her, for she had always been the more athletic of the pair, the more equipped for the rigors of heroism—Kade struggled to keep up. The bracken and briars that seemed inclined to let her pass unhindered snagged at the hems of his jeans. Holes opened beneath his feet, and he stumbled, he staggered, he swore. But he kept running. Sometimes, after all, that's what must be said to make a hero: the willingness to keep running even after it becomes clear that the entire exercise is doomed to failure. Sometimes heroism is pressing on when the ending is already preordained.

Cora ran, and Kade pursued, until the windmill was a speck in the distance, until it disappeared altogether, and there was only the Moors, and the glaring red eye of the moon, and the vast, alien darkness of the sea.

When Cora reached the cliff she stopped, wobbling at the very edge, chest heaving with the effort of breathing in the unforgiving air. Kade, gasping, staggered to a stop some fifteen yards behind her. He couldn't run any farther, and he tried to tell himself it was exhaustion, and he knew that he was lying, and he knew he was afraid.

"Wait," he wheezed, the word half-swallowed by his gasped attempts to breathe. "Cora, wait."

There was no way she could possibly have heard him. But she turned, and smiled, and it was the most beautiful expression he had ever seen. Heroes would have gone to war for that smile, would have died for even a shadow of its grace.

"It's all right," she said, and the wind carried her voice to him, each syllable polished and perfect as a pearl. "Can't you hear them? They've been waiting so long for me to come home. Tell Jack thank you, and that I forgive her. Tell her not to look for me."

"Cora, don't do this." Kade staggered forward, one

step, then another, trying to reach her before she did anything that couldn't be taken back.

"I'm home," she said, and stepped backward, over the edge, toward the welcoming sea. Her expression faltered—only for an instant, but long enough for Kade to see the terror in her eyes, shining through the glazed, artificial serenity.

He found he had the strength to run after all.

"*Cora!*" he howled, and dove toward the edge of the cliff. Too late, too late, too late.

She was already gone.

11 UNDER THE EAVES, WHERE SWALLOWS SLEEP

THE TOWN WAS oddly familiar. Christopher snapped his fingers as the gates swung closed behind them.

"I *knew* I'd seen this place before!" he said. "Didn't Vincent Price film a movie here?"

"Not everyone who visits the Moors decides to stay," said Jack.

"Are you saying Vincent Price—?"

"I'm saying there are a great many channels of cultural exchange between the worlds, and I'd prefer not to discuss them here, as drawing attention to ourselves is unwise."

"Says the girl with the skeleton horse," said Sumi.

Jack laughed.

The town really did look like something out of a black-and-white horror movie, for all that it was far from monochrome. The houses were painted in brilliant, eye-searing colors, making Sumi the only one who really matched the surroundings. There were little shops, public houses, even an inn with a sign advertising rooms to let. People walked along the narrow sidewalks flanking the street—if they could still be called "sidewalks" when they were made of wood instead of concrete. Christopher thought they might be boardwalks, or maybe promenades, but he wasn't sure. The nomenclature of architecture had never been his focus.

There was something faintly off about the people. Their eyes were too big and their fingers were too long and when they stopped to watch the wagon rolling by they were too perfectly, profoundly still, like predators lying in wait for their next meal. Sumi stared them down, and one by one they looked away, no longer willing to meet her eyes. She snorted.

"Not so brave after all," she said.

"Not under these circumstances," said Jack. "I advise against walking alone down any alleyways. I'm told the public house nearest the docks serves excellent chowder that practically never contains human flesh. I'm also told that 'practically never' is not the same as 'never,' and it's better not to gamble with such things. Anyone hungry?"

"I'm good," said Christopher hurriedly. Jack laughed. It wasn't a happy sound, not exactly; it was the sound of someone clinging to the last vestiges of sanity and stability with all their might. It was the sound of slipping.

Christopher shivered. No one who sounded that close

to the end of their rope could hold on forever. It simply wasn't possible.

The road led through the middle of town toward a towering edifice that appeared to be part cave and part cathedral. It had been carved from a single spire of blackened rock. Bells tolled in the distance, loud enough to have an almost physical presence.

And there, sitting on the edge of the wooden sidewalk, elbows on his knees and head bowed, was—

"Kade!" Sumi leapt down from the moving wagon and half-ran, half-skipped over to him, her oddly rollicking locomotion carrying her forward with startling speed. She stopped a few feet away, looking at him with a wide-eyed brightness that almost—*almost*—hid the wary caution in her eyes. "You ran away! *Bad* boy. Where's the mermaid?"

"She fell." He raised his head, looking through her more than at her, like he was staring at some distant, indescribable horizon. "She ran right to the edge of the world, and then she stepped off, and she fell. She didn't scream. She just *went*."

"The Drowned Gods called to her," said Jack, flicking the reins and urging the horses to a halt. "It was always a possibility. It's very sad, but we don't have time to sit around grieving when there's a monster to be defeated."

Kade stared at Jack for a single long, frozen moment. Then he lunged to his feet, grabbing her by the front of her shirt and yanking her off the wagon. She didn't fight him or resist. She just allowed him to pull her toward him, legs dangling, expression cold.

"I *warned* her," she spat. "I told her there were shadows in the sea, I told her the Drowned Gods might know her name, and she came anyway, because she didn't want to be left out of an adventure. This isn't an adventure to me. This is my home, my life, my *future*. I warned her and she came anyway. Break my sister's jaw if it makes you feel better. But be aware that there are worse things in the Moors than the sea, and all of them will come for you if I can't state my own challenge."

Kade grimaced. "You really are a monster," he said, and let her go.

Jack caught herself on the edge of the wagon, barely avoiding a tumble into the dust, and straightened up, adjusting her collar with unshaking hands. She kept her eyes on Kade the whole time.

"I never claimed to be anything else," she said, before climbing back into the driver's seat. "Come along. We've much to do, and time is short."

Kade and Sumi climbed into the back with Christopher. Jack flicked the reins, and they were away, continuing toward that blackened spire.

Red-robed acolytes appeared as the wagon neared its destination. They melted out of the nearby rocks with an air of casual, implacable menace. Hoods hid their faces, and their hands were empty, which was somehow worse than them being filled with weapons. Weapons, at least, were predictable; weapons made sense. A sword was just a knife with delusions of grandeur. A trident was a really big fork. This . . .

"What are they going to do to us?" asked Christopher.

"Nothing, unless they decide we've offended the Drowned Gods, which virtually never happens."

Kade made a wordless snarling sound. Jack ignored him.

"The Drowned Gods are amiable monsters," she said. "They sleep, and dream of worlds where fire is a forgotten impossibility, and occasionally they wake long enough to eat a few dozen villagers before going back to bed."

"Wait," said Christopher. "Are you saying they might *feed us* to their gods?" The question of whether the Drowned Gods might have eaten Cora was left mercifully unvoiced.

"Don't be silly," said Jack. "We haven't earned the honor." She pulled on the reins, bringing Pony and Bones to a halt, and called to the nearest acolyte, "Jack Wolcott, apprentice to Dr. Michel Bleak, and friends, here to see the High Priest about a little problem we're having. Will you please permit us to enter?"

The acolyte made a garbled hissing sound. Jack rolled her eyes.

"That may be so, but we don't have time for that, and your High Priest won't be pleased if you keep us here long enough to endanger my chances. There's a challenge beginning, and the entire protectorate is at stake. Your High Priest enjoys cheese, vodka, and fresh bread, none of which you're very good at making here. If no one buys your chocolate biscuits, how will he be able to purchase his necessary luxuries?"

The acolyte repeated the terrible hissing and stepped aside. The other acolytes followed suit. Jack nodded, pleased.

"I thought that might be your decision. Have a lovely evening." She flicked the reins, urging the horses toward the terrible maw of the black cathedral.

Sumi cocked her head. "Why is the village of scary fish-people where you get your chocolate biscuits?"

"It has something to do with shipwrecks and the tides, and to be quite honest, I don't know. Every time I ask Dr. Bleak, he tells me it's impossible to dissect the sea and orders me to leave it alone." Jack's face fell. "I suppose I'll have to learn, if we can't resurrect him. I suppose it'll fall on me to be the one who knows."

"A little knowledge never hurt anybody," said Sumi.

"Perhaps not. But a great deal of knowledge can do a great deal of harm, and I'm long past the point of having only a little knowledge."

Conversation died then, as the black cathedral swallowed them all alive. It didn't move in any way in the course of accomplishing this feat; it simply lay in wait, the perfect predator, and let them escort themselves through its jaws.

The stone closed in around them, moist and jagged and dripping, drops of seawater falling from the vaulted ceiling to land on their arms and in their hair. Dots of bioluminescence lit the walls and spangled the dangling stalactites, which hung like so many vast, sharpened teeth. Jack drove blithely on.

"Who *built* this place?" asked Christopher.

"That's a theological question," said Jack. "Science says no one built it: erosion and time did the bulk of the work, and then a few faithful stonemasons came in and cleaned up the rough edges to make it suitable for their liturgical needs. Faith says the Drowned Gods are ageless and eternal, and could very easily have shaped the course of erosion while in this area, guaranteeing their faithful a place to worship."

"What do you think?" asked Sumi.

"I think it's not my place to comment on someone else's religion. Science is my god. Lightning is my miracle, and storm clouds are my catechism. I don't need anything else to give purpose to my days. I find my purpose in the scalpel's shine, and the knowledge that I'm doing exactly what I was put in this world to do."

Sumi gave Jack an approving look. "You're like unnerving fudge with a chewy creepy center. School is a lot more boring without you there."

"Perhaps, but I wager there have been fewer murders." They had reached a rickety wooden suspension bridge, stretched across a canyon wide enough to almost qualify as an abyss. Jack pulled the horses to a stop again. This time, she tied off the reins before sliding out of the wagon and announcing, "We walk from here. Follow me, and try not to plummet to your deaths."

"Ha, ha," said Christopher flatly. When Jack didn't laugh, he frowned. "That was a joke, right?"

"I'm not a comedian," said Jack.

"We should at least go one at a time," said Christopher. "That doesn't look entirely stable."

"We can't." Jack gave him one of those unnervingly anxious looks, the ones that seemed to be ticking off her remaining capacity to cope. "Splitting up here, this close to the Drowned Gods . . . when they feed, they feed on the unprotected. We go together, or we're likely to disappear alone."

"That's fun," said Sumi.

"I'm well aware of the situation, thank you," said Jack, and stepped out onto the bridge.

It was narrow enough to sway with every step she took, and while there were rails, of a sort, they were made of braided rope, and didn't seem nearly sturdy enough to keep her from losing her balance and falling to the water below. The water *far* below: the drop from the bridge to the surface looked to be around eighty feet, and there were . . . things . . . writhing in those depths, things that would have looked like the arms of an octopus, if not for the fact that each of them was easily as big around as Cora's torso.

"This is terrible," said Sumi brightly. "I mean, we knew it was going to be terrible when we followed a mad scientist and her dead girlfriend to a horrifying murder world, but this is *bonus* terrible. This is the awful sprinkles on the sundae of doom." She skipped out onto the bridge, not seeming to care when it twisted and swayed under her feet. Christopher followed, his bone flute already in his hands, fingers moving through silent arpeggios to calm his nerves.

Kade was the last to leave solid ground for the swaying causeway. As bad as the bridge had looked from solid ground, it was worse. It shifted. It shook. The boards were damp from the ocean air, and his feet slipped and slid with every step, making him cling even harder to the ropes. If he missed a step, he'd fall, and if he fell—

He was so focused on keeping his balance that he didn't hear the board crack beneath his feet until it fell away and he was dangling over empty air, his grasp on the ropes the only thing keeping him from falling. He screamed, high and bright and clean, all of his terror and all of his resignation expressed in a single sound.

"Kade!" Christopher turned and bolted back to his position, dropping to his knees on the rickety wood and grabbing for his arms. "Take my hands! Don't let go!"

The two commands seemed contradictory: to take his hands, Kade would *have* to let go, have to risk that split second when he wasn't holding on to anything. Still, he started to loosen his grip, willing to gamble everything on how quickly they both could move, and was on the verge of reaching for him when the board Christopher was kneeling on snapped in two. Sumi grabbed the back of his shirt, dragging him to safety before anything worse could happen, and Kade was left dangling alone, surrounded by nothing but empty space.

"Kade!" shouted Christopher.

"It's all right," said Sumi, helping Christopher to his feet. She kept her eyes on Kade. "He's a hero too, remember? We're all heroes here. Sometimes a hero has to fall."

The words were needles, red-hot and sharp as anything. Kade closed his eyes. If he held on, the others would keep trying to save him—even Jack, who looked lost and scared, as if this change to her plan were already too much to stand. She was more fragile than anyone remembered her being, faced with the loss of home and mentor and even her own skin. She was falling apart, and Kade was just . . . falling.

If he stayed where he was, the others would kill themselves trying to do the impossible, and in the end, he'd fall anyway. That wasn't what a hero would do. That had never been what a hero would do.

He was never going to make it back to the school, never going to take over for Aunt Eleanor. He felt bad about that. By letting go, he would become one more person who let her down. But he didn't have a choice. Not anymore.

"Don't worry," he said. "Cora's waiting for me."

Then he let go.

He fell like a star, closing his eyes so he wouldn't be tempted to look back up and see his friends growing smaller and smaller on the bridge, which was still intact enough to get them where they needed to go. He was the only sacrifice it had demanded, and he didn't want to take their faces to his grave.

He fell, and the arms of the water were there to open wide and drag him down, without a sound, into the depths of the sea.

12 ALL THE DROWNED CHILDREN

CHRISTOPHER'S SCREAM WAS barely more than a howl. He moved toward the hole in the bridge and Jack was suddenly there, grabbing his arm. He turned to stare at her. She shook her head.

"No," she said. "You will *not*."

"Kade—"

"Kade is with Cora in the hands of the Drowned Gods now. Live or die, he does it at their whim, and your intervention will not change their decision. We need to move before this damned bridge dumps the rest of us in after them. Or do you think you're a better swimmer than the Goblin Prince and the former mermaid?"

"Not former," said Sumi. "Cora wears her scales on the inside now, that's all. Once you've been a mermaid, you'll always be a mermaid. You can't help it."

If Jack had been the first to turn away, things might have gone very differently. Jack could be cold; Jack could be heartless; Jack would always, always prioritize Jack above almost anyone else. That didn't make her a bad person, necessarily—practicality and pragmatism had their places, and as long as people never forgot that Jack would choose what was expedient over what was compassionate, she could be perfectly lovely company. But if she had been the first to give up, Christopher might have insisted on staying and trying to figure out a way to get Kade back, even as the bridge fell to pieces around him.

Instead, it was Sumi who bounced onto the balls of her feet, announced, "We have so much to do, and so little time to do it in," and turned to run, fleet as anything, to the far end of the bridge, where it joined back up with solid ground.

"She's right," said Jack, surprisingly gentle, and followed after Sumi at a more sedate pace.

Christopher stayed where he was for another count of ten, silently willing a head to break the surface of the water.

It didn't happen.

Christopher glared at the water. He glared at the broken bridge. And when he finally followed the others, he was weeping, making no effort to stop or to wipe the tears from his cheeks.

The cavern formed a tall dome, with the bridge marking its widest point; once across, the ceiling dropped and the walls narrowed, forming a single corridor no more than fifteen feet from the bridge's end. Jack and Sumi were waiting at the mouth of the corridor. Jack looked at Christopher, expression grave.

"From here, say nothing unless you're directly questioned, and even then, if you can avoid giving answer, do," she said, voice low. "The high priest can be . . . tedious at times, and will look for a way to win without actually joining the game. Do you understand?"

"I don't like this," said Christopher.

"Nor should you: it's dreadful." Jack's eyes were dry. That made sense: death was as commonplace to her as breathing. Still, it was easy in that moment to hate her, just a little. This was all her fault. If she hadn't come back to the school, if she had just stayed in the Moors where she claimed she belonged . . .

But that wasn't fair. None of this was fair.

"I didn't come looking for someone to die for me," said Jack, voice low and far too calm. It wasn't serenity: it was rigid control holding her words in place, like shackles around every syllable. "I wanted help. I had nowhere else to turn. This was not my intention, and I will be sorry for it later, I will mourn our friends for all the nights of my life. First we have to *secure* those nights. If we fail, they died for nothing."

"If we succeed, they died for nothing," Christopher snapped.

"That's not true," said Sumi. She turned from her contemplation of the walls, bouncing on her toes, filled with the endless energy that had already made her the savior of a spun-sugar fantasyland, and would inevitably make her so again. "If we succeed, they died to save a world. Wouldn't you have died to save Mariposa? I would have died to save Confection. The only reason I'm sorry Jilly-Jill killed me is because my death was useless. I didn't save anything. I didn't even save *her*. Let Kade be a hero again. It might not be what he wanted, but it's what he earned, and people have to have the things they've earned for those things to *matter*."

Christopher sighed, deep and low and defeated. "This isn't fair."

Sumi blinked at him. "Whoever said heroism was *fair*?" she asked. "It's the unfairest thing of all. 'Come away, oh human child, and learn to swing a sword for the sake of people who've decided the thing you're best for is dying in their name.' We were lambs for the slaughter, all of us, and if we survived this long, it's not because we're special. Come on. Let's be heroes one more time."

She spun on her heel and scampered down the corridor. Jack looked at Christopher, anxious and strained. Christopher shook his head.

"Fine," he said. "Let's go save your world."

They walked on in silence, and if they were privately relieved, they didn't say so. Christopher plodded. Sumi danced, skipped, and spun, seeming to view this all as some great game. Perhaps it was a side effect of travel in Nonsense, Christopher thought, watching as she played a strange variant of hopscotch with the puddles on the path ahead of them. When even heroism was a game, nothing could be taken seriously, and even the most trivial of situations could end in violence at any time.

The tunnel ended in a vast natural cathedral, the ceiling dripping with stalactites and hung with strings of lights that looked like something from a construction site, too modern for the rest of the setting.

"We sell them generators," Jack murmured, before anyone could ask. "In a world powered by lightning, everyone desires electricity, if only for the sake of keeping up with the neighbors."

At the far end of the vast room was a dais, and on the dais was a chair crafted from the helm of a great sailing ship, crusted with barnacles and candy-colored corals, until it became a gaudy monument to the sea, a carnival extraction dredged up from the deeps. It was cushioned in rotten, salt-stained velvet, and on it lounged a boy around Jack's age. His skin was the salt-white of a body left too long in the water, and his hair was long, black, and tangled with strands of precisely placed kelp. His lips were painted the same color, and thick rings of charcoal surrounded his green, calculating eyes. Red-robed acolytes stood all around him.

The boy—the high priest, Christopher supposed, as it would be ridiculous to think the acolytes took turns lounging around trying to look seductive—was also dressed in red, but his clothing was cut in a more piratical than priestly style, echoed all the way to the tentacle-shaped red coral prosthetic that replaced the lower half of his left leg. No, Christopher corrected himself; not a prosthetic. The tentacle twisted of its own accord, turning over to reveal a single glistening sucker. Whether this was a mobility device or a magic trick gone wrong, the tentacle was as much flesh as the rest of the high priest.

"Well, well, well," said the high priest. There was a bubbling undertone to his words, like he was speaking from deep underwater. "Jacqueline Wolcott, come to visit after all this time—and Jillian Wolcott as well, if I'm not mistaken. Have you finally made amends with your sister, and decided to strengthen your familial bonds by becoming a single entity?"

"I'd banter, but I haven't the time, and you haven't the wit to keep up," said Jack. "Hello, Gideon. These are my friends. Christopher Flores, late of Mariposa, and Sumi Onishi, late of Confection."

"We're heroes," said Sumi, cocking her head as she considered the high priest. "You're not a hero, I don't think. But you're not from here, either. Are you?"

"I'm not," said Gideon. He sounded delighted. "What a wonderful pair of wanderers you've found, Jack! And I'm told the Drowned Gods have accepted your sacrifice."

Christopher stiffened. Jack put out a hand to stop him before he could even start to move.

"Then you know these are unique circumstances," she said.

"Unique? A power struggle in the Moors is hardly 'unique.' If anything, a stretch of time as long as you had without your sister trying to rip your pretty throat out with her teeth counts as 'unique.' This is no concern of me or mine."

Jack bit the inside of her cheek—her sister's cheek—until her heartbeat calmed enough to leave her certain her voice wouldn't shake. "I think it is," she said finally. "What do *you* consider ordinary about this situation?"

"It's my business to know everything that happens in the Moors. Your Dr. Bleak is dead, perhaps beyond resurrecting, and the Master intends to bring his daughter fully into the family under the full moon. I have little doubt your motley band of heroes will be enough to destroy the elder vampire, even as foolish sentiment stays your hand from slaying your sister. The balance will be maintained. The two of you will make excellent monsters, until something novel comes along to take your place. The Abbey will stand, the Drowned Gods will smash ships against our shore, and I'll trade you rum and chocolate biscuits for bread and jam. It's happened before."

"Ah, but you see, that's where you're wrong." Jack started to walk forward, suddenly smiling. Jill had always taken excellent care of her teeth, anticipating the day when they'd become the symbol of her power. In the dimness of the Drowned Abbey, they gleamed. "I realize the Moors aren't very considerate when it comes to matters of mental health; I suppose when your power structure depends on the actions of scientists with poor impulse control and a variety of personality disorders, investing in therapy seems like a poor idea. But it's your job to know things, as you say, and so I'm sure you know that I've always had a bit of a problem with the filth of daily existence."

"I know you're squeamish, but you're bloody-minded enough to overcome it," said Gideon.

"No. I'm not. I have a condition—there isn't a word for it here, although I've heard a few of the older villagers comment about a cousin or grandparent with symptoms similar to mine—that transcends squeamishness. I can't abide being dirty. It revolts me. This body is tainted, Gideon. It's rotten, it's *spoiled*. The things my sister used it to do . . . I could wash the skin from these hands and still be unable to stand the sight of them. How do I wash my blood? My organs? How do I scrub the sins from my sister's skeleton?"

Gideon sat up straighter, looking alarmed for the first time. "I don't—"

"There's a natural balance between mad scientists and vampires, but I won't be a mad scientist for long. This will *break me*. This is already breaking me. My mind is eating itself alive, and only knowing my failure will mean the end of everything I love is letting me hold myself together." Jack took another step forward. "I'm a brilliant scientist, not despite my condition, but in some ways because of it. That does *not* mean I can survive under these conditions. So ask yourself, if you would be so kind—ask your damned and Drowned divinities. How long can I live like this? And how long do the Moors maintain their balance without someone to stop my sister from drenching your world in every drop of blood she can wring out of it?"

Gideon gaped, momentarily stunned into silence.

And from behind them came a wet, terrible sound.

Sumi was the first to turn. Christopher the second. Jack didn't turn at all. She didn't need to see what stood behind them.

But for the others, ah: there was Cora, draped in the sodden rags of her clothing, which seemed to have been ripped and rent by some unspeakable claw, by some demon of the deep. Her skin, where it was exposed by the torn fabric, gleamed like mother-of-pearl in the Abbey's stark electric light, and her hair hung in wet, heavy curls that tangled around her arms and breasts like eels. Her eyes were black from side to side, and the others couldn't look at them for more than a few seconds without feeling the terrible urge to look away, sheltering themselves from the secrets swimming there.

Kade was cradled in her arms, shipwrecked refuse of a softer sea.

"The balance must be maintained," she said, and her voice both was and was not her own. If a storm could have been said to have a voice, if a shipwreck could have spoken, it would have been the voice that dripped like poisoned pearls from Cora's lips. "The Moors are made of petty conflicts: they thrive on familial blood. But those conflicts can never matter more than the foundations themselves. The Drowned Abbey stands with Jacqueline Wolcott in the matter of her sister's malfeasance, and will help her to recover that which has been stolen."

"Thank you," said Jack, with swift, undisguised relief. "I—"

"We are not finished," said the things speaking through Cora's body. At least they sounded amused, and not angry at the interruption. "There will, of course, be payment."

"Anything," said Jack.

"No," said Christopher sharply. "*Not* anything." He turned to Cora—the Drowned Gods—whatever she was now, and said, "We get our friends back. Both of them. They're not yours to keep."

"Aren't they?" Not-Cora cocked her head. "They fell, voluntarily or no. The depths are ours. Everything within them belongs to us. The water knew this one, and she knew the water, and she breathed it willingly in."

"She isn't of the Moors," said Jack.

Not-Cora returned her terrible attention to the thin, damaged girl in the black leather gloves. "So?"

"These depths are yours, but she belongs to a different sea, and that sea may have Drowned Gods of its own, and they may take umbrage at you claiming something for your own amusement that they've already marked as belonging to them. If the purpose of this exercise is maintaining the balance of the Moors, do you want to risk offending your alternates? I'm sure they couldn't possibly defeat you here, in the place of your power, but . . ." Jack offered a delicate shrug. "The people of your protectorate are fragile when compared to you."

"Greedy little things," chided Not-Cora. "We never intended to keep this precious pearl; do not think you've won something we treasured. Still, the payment will be due."

"No lives," said Sumi.

"One life," said Jack. The others turned to her. She didn't move, but continued staring levelly at the things in Cora's skin.

"My sister," she said. "Jill can't walk away from this. I would never be safe. *Alexis* would never be safe. I killed her once, to save people I cared about but didn't love. To save the people I love, I'd destroy her so completely it would be as if she had never existed."

"Without her existence, the Moon would never have seen fit to send you a door," said Not-Cora.

Jack shrugged. "So I would have grown up innocently loveless, and never known what I was missing. I'll pay you with my sister's life. Is that enough?"

"Almost," said Not-Cora. The strangeness in her voice grew stronger, like the tide rolling in. "Almost. You'll stay, Jack of the Moors, Jack of the lightning. You'll stay until the Moon releases you from service. Not merely on the Moors, not merely in this world, but in your windmill, chained to your lightning and your learning as Dr. Bleak was before you, and Dr. Ghast before him, and Dr. Frost before her. If your lover leaves you for another protectorate, you will not follow. You will be the cruel light to balance the killing dark, and you will know, every day, that you have no choice. You belong to us now."

There was a moment of weighted silence before Jack laughed.

"Is *that* all?" she asked. "Yes. Yes, and yes, and yes again. I'll pay for your help by doing what I was raised to do, what I *want* to do, and I won't be sorry, not one minute, because this is who I am. I'm Jack Wolcott. I am the mad scientist who lurks in the fens and the fields, and I'll be *damned* before I'll let my sister take this world away from me."

The Drowned Gods smiled with Cora's lips, bowed Cora's head, and said, "Gideon. Gather the acolytes. High tide is coming." Then they opened her mouth and vomited black water across the Abbey floor in a terrible gout. Small fish thrashed there, and other, less comprehensible forms. Cora's eyes rolled up into her head and she collapsed, face-first, into the mess, dropping Kade in the process. He hit the ground and started coughing, knocking the water out of his own lungs.

"That was interesting," said Sumi, as Christopher

rushed to Cora. She bounced thoughtfully onto her toes before walking over to Gideon. She didn't say a word, merely stared at him until he squirmed on his rotted velvet cushion.

"What do you want, candy girl?" he asked.

"You," she said bluntly. "I have a true love, but he doesn't know I'm coming back, and there's no sense in staying celibate until we're together. All that can happen later, though. You have to help us now."

"I suppose I do," said Gideon, as Cora coughed the last of the black water from her lungs, as she clung to Kade like she feared drowning in the open air. Her skin still glistened with oily rainbows, but her eyes were her own again.

"And after, if there's time, before we go, I'll show you how we plough the fields in a world made of sugar." Sumi's smile was guileless and wicked at the same time. "It'll be nice."

"I suppose it will," said Gideon, as Jack reached for Cora's wrist, clearly intending to take the other girl's pulse, and had her hand swatted away. He smiled a bit, seeing that. There were always costs, always consequences, when the Drowned Gods chose to speak.

Jack, rebuffed, turned her attention back to Gideon. "When do we ride?" she asked.

"When the tide shifts," he replied. "If we're to ride with the blessing of the Drowned Gods, we'll do it when their power is at its greatest. You'd best be nice to me now, Jacky-my-girl. It looks like we're going to be neighbors for a long, long time."

"Only if we win," said Jack.

Gideon laughed. "Did you forget? I never lose."

Jack's expression, always sober, turned grim. She looked at Gideon levelly, until he squirmed in his throne and had to fight the obvious urge to turn away.

"I'm counting on that," she said.

Silence fell, save for the thin, gasping sound of Cora's sobs, and the distant, untamable roaring of the sea.

13 THE BROKEN CROWN

JACK SAT RAMROD straight in the driver's seat of the wagon, reins clutched in her gloved hands, hair braided so tightly that it became a measuring stick for her posture, sketching the line of her spine. She kept her eyes on the horizon, and on the growing shape of a small village protected by a vast wall, huddled in the shadow of a castle like a fawn seeking protection in the jaws of a lion.

Sumi lounged next to her, perfectly relaxed. She'd managed to acquire a wicked-looking baling hook from somewhere inside the Drowned Abbey and was using it to pick her fingernails, seemingly unconcerned by the fact that it was a rusty piece of metal large enough to pierce her entire hand.

Christopher and Kade sat to either side of Cora in the bed of the wagon, their shoulders hunched, tense, protective. There was no ocean here, no way for her to drown again, but her skin gleamed with rainbows, and no matter how much water ran from it, her hair never seemed to dry. They knew how close they'd come to losing her. Her and Kade both.

Cora said nothing as they rode, only gazed back at the shimmering line of the sea, and shivered, and clutched her fingers in the tatters of her shirt like she could serve as her own anchor, her own rocky shore.

Behind them came the acolytes of the Drowned Abbey, with Gideon at their head, seated astride a creature risen from the briny depths that was something like a great black frog, and something like a terrible fish, and something like nothing that had ever been intended to walk beneath the Moon. The luminous lure sprouting from between its bulbous eyes dangled in front of its terrible maw, sending glints of light dancing across its teeth. Gideon's sedan chair was affixed to the creature's back, and he rode with the comfortable ease of someone who knew that the most terrible of potential fates was in front of him, aimed at someone else.

Further back, behind the silent, hooded acolytes, who carried barnacle-encrusted swords and left trails of saltwater behind them, like they carried the sea itself in their pockets, came the villagers from the nameless settlement that lay beneath the Abbey. To be a villager on the Moors was to be a pawn in the long, slow game of life and death played between monsters, and they knew what was expected of them. They marched with grim expressions on their faces and the tools of their trade in their hands, baling hooks and fishing spears and tridents. Some of their number carried torches as well. Fire and water stood in opposition, but the casual reminder that most things could be flammable under the right circumstances was tradition, and tradition had a large part to play in this encounter.

Jack held the reins but didn't move them, trusting Pony and Bones to know the way, and tried not to think of Alexis, alone in the windmill, waiting for her to come home. Alexis wouldn't care if Jack won or if she lost, only that she survived, and Jack wished she could be that generous with herself; wished, with a fierce inner loathing, that she could be that generous for Alexis. If they failed to get her body back, she was going to break. Maybe not tonight, maybe not for weeks or even months, but she could feel the fault lines forming, could barely fight the urge to score her sister's unwanted flesh with her fingernails, trying to scrape enough of it away that she could find the cleanliness buried somewhere deep within.

They had to win. If they lost, even if she lived, she died, and it would be the kind of death that lightning couldn't save her from. They had to win.

Clouds gathered overhead, obscuring the great red eye of the moon. In the distance, thunder rolled, and a cold wind swept across the Moors, rattling the brush and chilling the flesh of the marchers. Jack flicked the reins, keeping her eyes only on their destination.

"It will be all right," said Sumi. "People will die or

they won't, but either way, it's almost at an ending, and things that are almost at an ending have a way of making their opinions known."

"If that was meant to be comforting, you're worse at this than I am," said Jack.

"Not comforting; comfort comes later. How well do you know Gideon?"

"He was here before me. His door dropped him on the seashore. I suppose the Moon makes some of our choices for us, and then everyone tries to pretend that She didn't. That's the trouble with gods. They don't care much how poorly they treat their toys."

"Mmm. Does he like girls?"

That was enough to startle Jack into looking Sumi's direction. The other girl was still picking her fingernails, but she was watching Jack out of the corner of her eye.

"I don't know," said Jack. "I never asked him."

"He's pretty."

"I've noticed that much, yes, but by the time he became High Priest—thanks to the previous High Priest having an unfortunate accident involving an unsecured widow's walk and a long plummet into an unwelcoming sea—and was hence free to court, I was already with Alexis, and I find monogamy unhygienic enough. Imagine needing to maintain a grooming regime for multiple partners." Jack shuddered delicately. "He's pretty, he's poisonous, and he's yours, if you want him. Leave me out of it."

"You're not my type," said Sumi.

Jack laughed—a single harsh, mirthless bark—and as if that were the cue for the distance to distort, the walls of the village loomed in front of them, too close too quickly. They were locked against the gathered darkness. Spots of fire glowed from the top, marking the position of the watchmen.

"I believe this is my cue," said Jack. She adjusted her glasses, took a deep breath, and called, in a voice gone suddenly sonorous, like the weight of the Moors lay across her shoulders, "I am Jacqueline Wolcott, apprentice to Dr. Michael Bleak, come to answer the challenge set against my house. Open your gates and let us pass. Our quarrel is not with you."

"Does that *work*?" asked Christopher, from the back of the wagon. "Why would these people just let us in when we're here to fight their big bad boss?"

"Because we have an army, and they enjoy their homes being unburnt," said Jack. Her gaze didn't waver from the wall. "You have to be at least a little bloody-minded to survive here. They know their Master won't reward them for defending him. That isn't how a challenge works. All they can do is die for a man who's never viewed them as anything more than cattle. It would be senseless."

As if to prove her point, the gates creaked open. Jack nodded to herself, gathering the reins.

"They are, however, likely to attempt to pour pitch or

oil on us, so we'll be going through as quickly as—yah!"
She flicked the reins as she shouted. Pony and Bones, not
bound to the physical limitations of ordinary flesh-and-
blood horses, recognized this for the challenge it was and
took off at a run so fast that it felt, for a moment, as if
the wagon might come apart from the strain.

They dashed through the open gates directly ahead of
a sheet of bubbling liquid that caught fire when it hit the
ground. It clung to the cobblestones marking the edge of
the village, burning. Cora and Kade watched with wide,
horrified eyes as the acolytes of the Drowned Gods continued marching. Gideon raised his hand in a careless
wave. The storm, which had been threatening for some
time, descended. The sky tore, and water sheeted down,
extinguishing the flames.

The rain was localized, and stopped as quickly as it
had started. Kade squinted, and realized he could still
see the torches held by the marching villagers, untouched
by the downpour.

"I don't think I like this place," he said, and Cora
began to giggle uncontrollably, still clinging to his arm.

"No one does," said Jack, slowing the horses. "Either
you love it here or you hate it here. The Moors have little
time for shades of gray."

"That's no way to live," said Kade.

"It's a very effective way to die," said Jack, and urged
the horses on, an army behind them, the village to all
sides. Curtains twitched as people peered out into the

street, saw what was happening, and withdrew again, back into the safety of their homes, away from the coming chaos. Jack smirked.

"He's never used anything but fear to buy their loyalty. They're afraid of being murdered in their beds, of seeing their children transformed into monsters, and those are good, reasonable fears—"

"We have different ideas of 'reasonable,'" muttered Christopher.

"—but they aren't enough to make his people rise up in his defense. If we lose, nothing changes. They still live in fear. If we win, maybe things get better, for a while. Fighting does nothing, so they won't fight."

"Charming," said Kade.

Jack laughed and drove on, the forces of the Drowned Abbey behind her.

They traveled the length of the village, and when they reached the lower walls of the castle, Jack stopped the horses and slid down, patting Pony's flank before she turned to the others. The army marched on, heading for the long, winding road up to the castle. Gideon looked over at the group as he passed, and he winked, seeming pleased by their abdication of the vanguard.

"There's a door," Jack said. "It's meant to be hidden, but I know the way."

"Why?" asked Sumi.

"The Master wanted me for his daughter, once. He would have killed Jill if he'd been allowed to have me.

So I left, through the hidden door, in the company of Dr. Bleak. It was the first time I saved my sister." She tugged her gloves more securely into place. "I've saved her three times now. I suppose that means I've met my quota. Come along."

She walked the length of the wall, stopping at a stone that looked like all the stones around it. She reached up and pushed it, and it slid inward with a soft click. A door swung open in what should have been solid stone.

On the other side was a woman. She was thin and pale and hunched in on herself, like she feared the consequences of taking up too much space. Her hair was a Medusa's nest of tangled brown curls that seemed almost to move of its own accord; her eyes were the color of dishwater, and so very tired. She looked at Jack. Jack looked at her, both silent for the measure of a moment.

Finally, Jack said, "You're younger than I remember you being. I thought . . ." She stopped.

The woman almost smiled. "You were a child," she said. "To a child, anyone old enough to be in high school is ancient. I'll be thirty in the fall, if I survive this day's work. Old enough to know what I'm dying for. Tell me why you're here, girl who chose to leave us."

"This is portentous and all, but can we hurry things up?" Christopher glanced at the sky, where black clouds loomed. "I don't like the looks of that storm."

"I do," said Jack, eyes still on the woman. "The Master and Jill came to our home. They attacked Dr. Bleak.

They attacked me. A challenge has been issued for balance of this protectorate, and I'm within my rights to answer."

"It looks like you've answered with a frontal assault."

"I have. They'll storm the gates, break into the hall, fight the Master's servants. Some of them will die. I'll resurrect as many as I can, once this is over." Jack sounded unconcerned. It would have been chilling, if she hadn't also sounded so tired. "Perhaps they'll even face the Master, although there's not much chance they'll kill him, not when the Drowned Gods haven't come out of the sea. I'm here for my sister."

The woman nodded. "What will you do if you find her? I know what she did to you." Her lips twisted. "I brushed her hair and tied her stays for years. There was no way I'd miss the fact that she's in a body not her own."

"I'll take back what belongs to me," said Jack. "And once I'm secure in my own skin, I'll kill her. Please, Mary. Let us pass."

Mary nodded and stepped aside. Jack was almost through when Mary's hand shot out and grasped her wrist, hauling her to a stop.

"Everyone who comes here becomes a monster: you, me, your sister, everyone," said Mary, voice low and fast and urgent. "The doors only open for the monsters in waiting. But you made the right choice when you left this castle, because you would have been the worst monster of them all if you had grown up in a vampire's care."

"I know," said Jack, and twisted her wrist free, and walked on.

The others followed her, first Sumi, then Kade and Cora. Christopher brought up the rear, bone flute in his hand and shadows in his eyes. Too many of the children at school had called his door, his world, monstrous, but he'd never really known what that meant: not until this place, with its shadows and its secrets and its terrible, watching moon. Once he was through the door, Mary stepped outside and closed it behind her, and there was relief and sorrow in that motion, like she was doing something that couldn't be taken back.

Jack kept walking.

The corridor seemed to have been hewn from the very stone of the castle's foundations. The walls were slick with unspeakable fungus and foul liquids; the corners were packed with cobwebs, and while he couldn't be sure—didn't *want* to be sure—Kade thought he saw a spider the size of a rat scurrying behind the glittering film. Torches dotted the passageway, one roughly every ten feet or so, and the smell of fragrant smoke covered the other, less pleasant odors.

Kade walked a little faster, catching up to Sumi and nudging her, ever so gently, aside. She fell back to walk beside Cora. He matched his steps to Jack's, and waited.

"This is the only way," she said.

"Killing someone's not that easy," he said.

She laughed, low and bitter. "I already killed her once, remember?"

"With the intention of bringing her back. You're not going to do that this time, are you?"

"No." Jack shook her head. "It's not safe to have her stalking the battlements and planning another way to get my body. She has to die. I'll salvage what I can. I'll spread her organs throughout the Moors, give them to people whose lives will be bettered by her sacrifice, and maybe sometimes I'll see those people and think 'that man has my sister's heart, that woman has my sister's eyes, I didn't kill her completely; she still did something good, she's still here.' But Jill herself? The girl I shared a womb with, the girl who was meant to matter to me more than anything else? She dies tonight. In my body or her own, she dies."

Kade was quiet for a few moments before he said, "I could do it."

"You?" Jack glanced his way. "You're squeamish. You dislike the sight of blood. You couldn't help us melt the flesh from a corpse. No. I appreciate the offer, but no. My sister's death is my responsibility, and no one else's."

They had reached the base of a narrow stone stairway. Jack stopped, taking a deep breath, and turned to the others.

"It may seem hypocritical to do this now, but I feel I must offer you the opportunity to stay behind," she said. "You've been invaluable in getting me to this point. From here, I can continue alone."

"You won't win alone," said Sumi.

Jack inclined her head. "In all likelihood, no. But I'll feel less as if I've drawn my only friends to their doom. I'd prefer it if you accompanied me. I am . . . afraid. More so than I expected to be. One way or another, no one is going to refer to 'the Wolcott sisters' after tonight, because there won't be any. If I fail, if I fall, please take Alexis back to the school. She won't be safe here."

"We will," said Kade. "But you're not going to fail, and you're not leaving us behind."

"I drowned because of this girl," said Cora. "I'm seeing this through to the end."

Christopher said nothing, only nodded and ran his fingers along the flute he clutched so tightly in his hands.

Jack sighed, and smiled, and turned to begin the long, slow walk up the stairs, toward the castle heights, to where a vampire and his daughter waited.

14 CAME TUMBLING AFTER

THE STAIRS WENT on for the better part of what felt like forever, until all of them were plodding, and even Sumi had stopped trying to pick up the pace. When they finally reached the top, Jack paused, pressing one hand against her chest, and wheezed.

"Would it have *killed* her to go jogging once in a while?" she asked, a note of fear behind the peevishness. She was going into battle while wearing a body whose limitations she didn't understand and had no time to learn. "I swear, 'I'm going to become a deathless creature of the night' is not a substitute for a comprehensive fitness plan."

"Maybe you should let us go in first," said Kade.

Jack shook her head. "That's not how these things are done," she said.

"I never thought you were stupid," said Sumi. When Jack whipped around to glare at her, she shrugged.

"Doing something you know could get you hurt because it's how things are done isn't *smart*."

"Maybe not," said Jack. She sighed and straightened, her breathing leveling out. "But I have to live with myself when this is over, and that means I go in first." There was a crash beneath them. The castle shook on its foundations. The crack of thunder split the sky. There were no windows, but the air became harsh and electric, and they knew, every one of them, that the lightning had followed the thunder almost instantly, out of order and intentionally so, that the storm was perched directly above them.

Jack closed her eyes. Only for a moment; long enough to take a deep, ozone-laden breath.

"It's time," she said. "Thank you for coming this far."

Then she opened her eyes, and turned, and opened the door.

The room on the other side was opulent to the point of becoming ludicrous, a child's dream of a princess's life made somehow manifest. The bed was large enough to border on obscene, surrounded by hanging veils of lace and mounded with pillows and comforters. Wardrobes and dressers lined the walls, bulging with silks and satins and covered in heaps of discarded jewels, like pearls and garnets had no value beyond how many could be placed in a single pile. The floor was covered in thick rugs, hiding all trace of stone, and the rugs were covered in turn by pieces of clothing, idly tossed aside.

Jack stepped into the room alone and walked toward the bed, where a scrap of too-bright fabric poked out from under one of the pillows. She pulled it loose and held it up: a child's shirt, too small for any of them.

"She was wearing this when we found our door," she said, dropping the shirt back onto the bed. "Jill has never been good at letting go of the things she thinks belong to her. The things she thinks she deserves."

"This room is sort of . . ." Cora paused, trying to put her appalled thoughts into words.

"Excessive," said Sumi. "Coming from me, that means a lot."

"Yes, well. We made our choices when we were too young to understand them, and maybe she needed a little excess." Unspoken went the fact that if a little excess had been enough for Jill, none of them would have been standing here. She sighed. "We haven't been close in a very long time. The body I'm wearing knows this bed better than my heart knows my own sister."

Lightning flashed outside. The stained glass in the room's wide window broke it into a glittering rainbow of color, painting it across their skins. All of them felt the hairs on their arms and the backs of their necks as they stood on end. Jack walked to the door on the far wall and opened it, revealing a wider, brighter hallway than the one below.

"Come," she said, and walked on.

The sounds of fighting were audible once they were

in the hallway. They reached a split in the hall, and Jack went right, leading them to the base of another, shorter stairway. She reached up, untying her cravat. The scars on her neck stood out starkly, tiny white dots outlining the arch of her veins. She pulled the cravat free, wrapping it around her hand.

Without a word, she began to climb. The others followed, a step at a time. The air grew colder, and the scent of rain tickled their noses, until they emerged onto the high parapets of the castle. There, standing with her hands resting on the edge of the wall and the wind whipping her gown into a pale froth around her legs, was Jack's twin.

Jack stopped just inside the narrow chamber separating the castle from the storm. "Hello, Jill," she said, voice low and almost apologetic. "You know I don't like it when you touch my things."

"Do you mean your body or your precious *teacher?*" Jill turned, leaning languidly against the wall as she ran one bare hand down the slope of her side. "I can't apologize if you don't tell me which I'm apologizing for."

Christopher, who had never wanted to think of Jack like that, flushed and turned away. "Uncool either way, Jill."

"Christopher?" Jill sounded unaccountably delighted. "Kade! And—Sumi? Didn't I kill you already? I know things were a trifle hectic there toward the end, but I usually remember when I kill someone." Her attention flicked dismissively to Cora. "And you. Who are you?"

"You did," said Sumi. She twirled her baling hook, seemingly unconcerned. "I got better."

"You went back to school. Why, Jack, I didn't know you had it in you." Jill beamed. "See, we can all be happy: you can take your friends and go sit in math class washing your hands until all the skin comes off. I'll stay here and keep watch over the Moors with my father, forever."

"He's not your father," said Jack. She tilted her chin upward, exposing the soft, scarred skin of her throat— Jill's throat, really. Jill was the one who'd willingly submitted to a vampire's idea of love. "Would a father do this?"

"He's better than the one *you* have," snapped Jill.

"I don't know whether you mean Mr. Wolcott or Dr. Bleak, and I don't care," said Jack. "Mr. Wolcott was a fool who should never have had children. His genetic donation is noted and appreciated. Dr. Bleak is not my father, but he loves me, and he cared for me when no one else would, and you had no right to kill him. Where is his head, Jillian?"

"Oh, full names, now? Are you trying to remind me of the time when everyone thought you were the pretty one, and I was the useless extra?" Jill finally pushed away from the wall, taking a step toward the group. "He took you away. He deserved to suffer."

"Where is his *head*?"

"Where you'll never find it!" Jill balled her hands. "I'm going to be a vampire! I'm going to be happy! You've always taken everything from me! You don't get to take this, too!"

"Christopher," said Jack, "this is the sort of confrontation that always plays out better with a bit of musical accompaniment. If you'd be so kind?"

Christopher blinked. "But my flute—"

"*Please*," she hissed, through gritted teeth.

Christopher hesitated before he raised his flute to his mouth and began to play.

It didn't look like a functional instrument to the casual viewer. The "holes" were merely slight indentations in the surface of the bone; the chamber, while hollow, was neither regular nor polished. It was a Halloween decoration, a toy, and no matter how hard Christopher blew, it never made a sound.

Far below them, around the foundations of the castle, the bones of those who'd fallen from the windows trying to escape began to stir, pulling themselves together and rising on legs that lacked flesh or tendon, yet functioned all the same.

In nooks and crannies and sheltered spots throughout the castle proper, the Master's victims began to wake and rise, clattering through the building, heading for the parapets. Some were caught in the fighting that had broken into the ballroom from the entry hall, and they fell to pieces under swords and the furious thrusts of the servants, dying for a second time. Their unintentional sacrifices bought the attackers a few precious seconds, and they turned them to good use, cutting down the Master's faithful like so much poisoned wheat.

Christopher played and the skeletons marched, as Jack walked toward her sister beneath the shattered, stormy sky.

"I never tried to take anything from you, Jill," said Jack. "We were children. We didn't ask for any of this; we never did anything to deserve it. I left you here to protect you. The Master would have chosen me, and you would never have been safe."

"Because I needed your castoffs? Your *charity*?"

"Because you wanted to be taken care of!" Jack's words became a howl, half-drowned in the crash of lightning. She whipped her glasses off, squinting at her sister. "You wanted someone to pet you, and pamper you, and—and let you be fragile for a while! And I didn't! I was done being fragile. I wanted to have an adventure, I wanted to learn things and do things and not just be someone's precious trinket! Neither of us had any *choices*, Jill, we never got to be sure of anything! So I left you, because if I didn't choose to go, we were going to keep not choosing anything. I'm sorry. I failed to be your sister. I didn't realize you needed me. But that doesn't make it right for you to take whatever you want and act like no one else matters. People matter. *I* matter."

"Not for long, little spare," growled a voice.

Jack didn't turn. Kade and Sumi did. There, behind them in the entryway, loomed a tall, black-haired man in a red-lined velvet cloak. His shirt and teeth were almost blinding in their brightness. He smiled, showing the wicked points of those same teeth, and he lunged for Kade, hissing.

Sumi's baling hook caught him in the throat before he could reach the boy. "*Naughty* vampire," she said, hauling backward, piercing his trachea. "It's not nice to bite people you don't know. It sends the wrong message."

Kade yelped and scrambled backward, away from the Master's grasping hands. He stumbled over a chunk of broken masonry. Stooping, he grabbed it and slung it as hard as he could at the Master's face, hitting him squarely in the mouth. The Master howled. Sumi hauled on her baling hook again, keeping him from recovering his balance, while Kade grabbed more pieces of masonry and flung them, one after the other, like he thought he could win a prize if he hit the bullseye enough times. Cora rolled the largest chunks of stone she could find toward him, positioning them perfectly for his hand.

"This is fun," Sumi chirped. "I could do this all day."

"Father!" shrieked Jill, and ran toward the struggling vampire.

Jack stomped on the edge of her nightgown, jerking her to a sudden stop. Jill hissed and whirled around, reaching for her sister as the thunder rolled. Jack's body was stronger and faster, and Jill nearly had her hands around her sister's throat when Christopher's skeletons came boiling over the walls and swarmed the pair, grabbing only for Jill, dragging her back without dragging her away.

In the noise and chaos, it was understandable that the small, simple sound of Jack's glasses snapping in two went overlooked. She grabbed Jill's hand, tangling it in her carefully positioned cravat, until they were solidly tied together.

"I did love you," she whispered. "Please believe that much, if you can."

Then she thrust her free hand into the air, the broken arms of her glasses jutting from between her fingers, a makeshift lightning rod at the center of a storm. The lightning lashed down, a slash of bleeding white against the darkness, pouring itself into the metal, filling it from end to end with burning heat. The force of the blast scattered the skeletons, sending their individual bones flying in all directions. Jill howled. Jack screamed. And somewhere in the middle of that terrible, unbearable sound, the tones traded places. Jack started to lower her hand. Jill grabbed her elbow, forcing it back toward the sky.

No. That wasn't what happened. *Jill*, now dressed in Jack's clothing, now wearing her own body, tried to lower her hand, and *Jack*, now dressed in Jill's lacy gown, finally back in her own skin, forced her to keep it up, until the lightning died, until the two of them stood, shaken and smoking and alone.

Jill shrieked and dropped the molten remains of Jack's glasses, cradling her wounded hand to her chest. The metal had burned through the leather of Jack's glove. "It isn't *fair*," she whimpered. "You get *everything* and it isn't *fair* and I'll beat you, I swear I'll beat you, I swear I'll win next time, I swear—"

"You'll never give up," said Jack softly. She pulled her hand out of the loop formed by her own cravat and started pushing her sister inexorably toward the wall, using her own superior strength—the strength born from a lifetime of hard labor—to overcome Jill's vague attempts to struggle. "You'll keep coming, and coming, and coming, and hurting the people I love."

"Yes," spat Jill. "Until I *win*."

"The Moors turned us both into monsters," said Jack. The resignation in her tone was a roll of thunder, heavy and unforgiving. "But it did a better job with me."

Then she shoved Jill over the edge.

PART IV

A BETTER MONSTER

15 A HEART OF WIRE AND GLASS

JILL FELL WITHOUT a sound, her hair still smoking from the lightning, a wide-eyed, puzzled expression on her face, like this couldn't possibly be happening, not here, not to her; she was the heroine of the piece, and she was meant to walk away.

The Master finally ripped himself free of Sumi's baling hook. Before she could snare him again, he lunged, grabbing Jack by the shoulders, whipping her around to face him. The wound in his throat was already healing.

"What have you *done*?!" he demanded, shaking her. "You little—"

"Dr. Bleak is dead," said Jack. "Until I resurrect him—if you've left me enough to work with—I am your opposition and your equal. Unhand me, unless you wish the judgment of the Moors to be upon you."

Her voice was eerily calm for someone who'd just shoved her own sister from the castle wall.

The Master stared at her. Then, slowly, he released her, stepping back. "You killed my daughter," he said. "I will not forget this."

"She could have lived a long, long time if you hadn't insisted on finding a way to turn her into what you wanted her to be," said Jack. "She loved you so much. She would have done anything to please you."

"And you *killed* her."

"Yes. I'll live with that for the rest of my life, however long that happens to be. Where is Dr. Bleak's head, please?" Jack tilted her head, looking at him with polite anticipation. "This is an excellent storm. I'd like to take advantage of it."

"If you bring him back . . ."

"If I bring him back, I'll be vulnerable. I'm aware. Only one monster at a time, and all that. But you see, I love him, and children will do anything for their fathers. His head, please, and we'll be on our way."

The Master curled his lip in disgust. "You'll have your head. I knew you should have belonged to me," he said, and spun on his heel, and swept away.

"I wish there'd been time to get my gloves," said Jack, still in that impossibly level, impossibly calm voice. "I can take them once we recover the body, I suppose, but there's always the chance she's leaking on the leather. I'll have to scrub my hands with lye when I get back to the windmill. It's the only way to be sure."

"Jack?" Kade took a cautious step forward. "Are you . . . ?"

"There are only a certain number of possible ways to end that question, and the answer to all of them is 'no,'" said Jack. "No, I'm not okay. No, I'm not going to be okay. No, no, no. Everything is terrible. I've killed my sister. Again. I was always the monster at the end of her story, and she died knowing everything she thought about me was true." She shook her head. "I want to leave this place. Can we go?"

"Yeah," said Kade gently. "We can go."

They descended the stairs into the castle in the order that had brought them there: Jack, then Sumi, then Kade and Cora, and last of all Christopher, whose hands were finally still.

When they reached the hall outside Jill's room, Jack kept walking, bringing them to a wide interior stairway. Jill's nightgown flared out around Jack's feet with every step, and her hair was loose and wild, and she looked every inch the vampire's daughter, an illusion that was reinforced when every servant they passed shied away from her, terror in their eyes.

The sounds of fighting had long since stopped. When they reached the ballroom, they stepped into an abattoir. Bodies were strewn in all directions. Some wore the robes of the Drowned Abbey; some wore the Master's household livery. Others wore village clothing, and when

they fell face-down, it was impossible to tell whose village they had come from. Gideon sat in his chair at the
center of the room, his surviving people arrayed behind
him. The Master's surviving servants were backed into
the corner.

Jack strode toward him, barefoot in the gore, blood
and other terrible, viscous fluids soaking into the lacy
hem of her gown. She didn't seem to notice. Kade
flinched. If Jack didn't notice she was getting dirty . . .

Oh, this was bad. This was very, very bad.

"Well?" asked Gideon, as Jack drew closer. "Which
Wolcott are you? The fun one, or the scientist? Who
won?"

"I will slice you open and spread you as evenly as a
coat of jam across the shore," said Jack levelly. "I'm sure
the Drowned Gods will forgive me, since I've agreed to
stay and maintain the balance for their sake."

"Ah," said Gideon. "The scientist. We won, too."

"Bully for you." Jack turned to face the stairs as the
Master came sweeping down, a burlap sack in his hand.
"Excellent. We'll be leaving now."

The Master snarled, showing her his teeth, but didn't
argue; merely flung the sack containing Dr. Bleak's head
into the blood and fluids on the floor. Jack gathered it
without a word of complaint, holding it, dripping, to her
chest. She turned back to Gideon.

"I won't forget you helped me," she said. "Give me
from this full moon to the next to get my house in order,

and then send me anyone you have who requires medical care. I'll rob a few graves if I have to, but I'll fix them for you, free of charge. Just this once."

"Just this once," agreed Gideon, with the ghost of a smile.

Jack inclined her head and walked away without another word.

"Should we follow her?" asked Cora.

"She *is* the only one who knows how to make us a door home, and I don't want to live here," said Christopher. "My girlfriend is a literal skeleton, and this is too creepy for me."

They followed as Jack left the ballroom, pulled down a sconce, and walked through the hidden door that opened in the opposing wall. They followed her down the stairs, back to the place where they had entered the castle.

Pony and Bones waited outside. Pony was chewing on something that looked like a chunk of raw meat. None of them looked any closer. Instead, Jack dropped the bag containing Dr. Bleak's head on the seat before she turned and walked further around the base of the castle, Sumi and Christopher behind her, while Kade and Cora remained with the wagon.

When they found Jill, she wasn't moving. She had landed in a graceless sprawl, and it was clear, when Jack and Christopher gathered her up and lifted her, that several things inside her body had broken so profoundly that they could never be repaired, not even here, where science could do virtually anything. Sumi folded Jill's hands across her chest, and the three of them carried her back to the wagon like pallbearers at the world's least-attended funeral. They lay her down in the hay, and Jack climbed silently into the driver's seat, leaving the others to arrange themselves.

This time, Kade rode up front, while the others—who were less squeamish, or maybe just more accustomed to this world and its horrors—rode in the back. He glanced at Jack as she drove. She didn't glance back. Her eyes were fixed on the fields ahead, and the bag containing Dr. Bleak's head rested in her lap like a swaddled child, something to be cared for and protected.

When the windmill came into view ahead, Kade swallowed. "Jack—" he began.

"Don't." Her voice was still utterly, eerily calm. "Please."

He didn't.

Jack drove on.

When they were close enough to the windmill to see details—the slope of the fence, the narrow, shuttered slits of the windows—the back door opened, spilling buttery yellow brightness into the darkness. Alexis appeared, silhouetted in the lamplight. Jack managed to contain herself long enough to pull the horses up to the stable. Then she jumped down and ran to the other woman, the burlap sack held in one hand. She flung herself into Alexis's arms, and neither of them said anything, and neither of them had anything to say.

Kade looked awkwardly away. "Any of you know anything about horses?"

"No, but I know skeletons," said Christopher. "Let's get to work."

By the time they finished unhitching the horses— Pony nipped, while Bones was docile as could be—and returning them to their stalls, Alexis was alone in the doorway. The four of them approached her cautiously.

She raised her hands and signed something. Sumi nodded.

"Jack went upstairs to change her clothes," she said. "She'll be right down, and then they'll send us home. Alexis says thank you, by the way. She wasn't sure we'd be back. She knew Jack couldn't do it on her own."

Alexis signed something else.

"She's sorry we had to see that," Sumi said. "She's sorrier Jack had to do it. She hoped . . ." Sumi stopped, and glared at Alexis. "That's not nice."

"What did she say?" asked Cora.

"She hoped one of us would kill Jill, so Jack wouldn't have to." Sumi crossed her arms and pouted, her petulance only slightly spoiled by the fact that she was still holding the baling hook.

"I offered," said Kade.

Cora looked at her hands, still covered in mother-of-pearl, and said nothing.

Alexis stepped to the side, an apologetic look on her face. Jack was descending the stairs, a fresh pair of glasses on her face, buttoning the cuffs of her shirt.

"I suppose you'd like me to send you home," she said.

"That'd be nice," said Kade.

"I don't suppose I can convince any of you to stay behind." Jack smiled, quickly enough that it could almost have been missed. "We have plenty of room here in the windmill. I could teach you the finer points of grave robbing."

"I don't think this world touches on Confection," said Sumi.

"Even if this world touches on Mariposa, it's a pass for me," said Christopher. "This place is not right."

"No," said Kade.

"I want to," said Cora.

They all turned to look at her.

"The Drowned Gods keep whispering to me, and this isn't the Trenches, but they could give me back the sea," she said. "Gideon is . . . he stays dry too much. They'd give me the sea, and then they'd give me his place, and I'd be so important, I'd be so beloved, and I can't, I *can't*, this isn't . . . this isn't my home, this isn't . . ."

"Cora." Kade took her hands, pulling her attention onto him. She raised her head, blinking rapidly, eyes swirling with impossible colors. Kade forced himself to smile. "Hey. We're pretty fond of you back home, you know. We love you. But if this is . . . maybe this isn't the home you had, but maybe it could be a new home. Maybe you could have the ocean back, and be happy. It's all right if you want to stay. We'll tell my aunt. She'll understand."

Cora stared at him, cheeks slowly reddening as she squirmed under the weight of his regard. Then, with an effort that looked physically painful, she shook her head.

"No," she said. "If the Trenches want me back, they'll come for me. I don't want someone else's sea. I want my own. I want to go home."

"All right." Kade looked over his shoulder to Jack. "Fire it up, do whatever you need to do. Send us back."

She nodded, regret flashing in her eyes. "Very well, then. I suppose we won't see each other again. Thank you for your assistance. Please tell Miss West that I . . . that I appreciated my time with her."

Kade nodded. "We will."

They stood back as Jack and Alexis assembled the components of the door. From this side, it was a structure of wire and steel, sketching a doorway where none belonged. Jack flipped a switch. Lightning filled the room, and when it cleared, a door was standing there, solid oak.

Christopher licked his lips. "If you can make doors . . ."

"Only between the Moors and the world of my birth," said Jack. "If you'd like to remain and go through an apprenticeship, you might be able to make yourself a doorway home. But I doubt it. Science has limits, even here. Go back to school. Live until you find your door, or until you don't. Be happy. Be sure."

"I'll try," said Christopher, and opened the door, and stepped through.

Cora was the next through. Sumi paused long enough to blow Jack a kiss and then danced after the former mermaid, her steps light, her baling hook hanging lazily at her side.

Kade hesitated. "Jack . . ."

"Please don't," she said. "Crying is very untidy, and I can't handle any more mess today."

"I'm glad you came to us for help," he said. "We miss you."

Jack managed a smile. "I miss you too. But I'm happy here. This is where I belong. Alexis and I . . . we're going to raise a family. What's the point of knowing how to pervert science to your own ends if you can't use it selfishly every once in a while?"

Kade laughed. Then he pulled her into a hug, careful not to touch any of her exposed skin, and whispered, "You're not a monster."

"Oh, but I am," said Jack. "I'm just . . . a good one."

Kade let go. He gave her one final look before nodding to Alexis and stepping through the door. It slammed shut behind him, and he found himself standing in the basement with the others. He turned. The door was gone.

"Well," said Christopher. "That happened."

"It sure did," said Kade. "You okay?"

Christopher started to answer. Then he paused, wrinkled his nose, and said, "I left my good jeans back in the mad science windmill."

Sumi laughed, high and bright and utterly sincere, and things were going to be all right. Not the same as they had been, maybe; nothing is ever the same after an adventure, after someone dies. But all right, and maybe that was just as good, in its own quiet way.

"I'm going to tell Ely-Eleanor that we're back!" said Sumi, and went galloping up the stairs, still carrying the baling hook.

Kade's eyes widened. "Sumi, slow down!" he shouted, chasing after her. "You're going to trip and impale somebody!"

Christopher and Cora exchanged a look.

"This school is weird," she said.

"You're covered in rainbows," he said.

"That's pretty weird," she said. "Good thing I go to school here."

Christopher grinned. "Good thing."

They followed their friends up the stairs, leaving the basement—and the electrical burns on the concrete floor—behind them.

EPILOGUE
WRITE YOUR NAME IN LIGHTNING; SHAME THE SKY

THE SKY WAS black with clouds and white with flashes of lightning. The bloody face of the Moon stole glimpses of the land below whenever the wind ripped holes in the outline of the storm, keeping watch over it all.

Far below, in a windmill, two girls—both old enough to be women now, if they wanted to be, but clinging with all their might to the shattered shreds of their childhoods, which had been torn away from them too soon—arrayed a body on a slab. He had been a big man, before death made him smaller. His head was attached to his body by clever, secure stitches made of stretched tendon, intended to keep it there long enough for him to heal. His arms and legs were strapped down. Cables ran from every part of his body to a vast lightning rod, which was connected in turn to a generator powerful enough to run a city.

Jack stepped up next to the slab, reaching over to gently, tenderly brush his hair away from his eyes.

"I lied to Jill," she said. "I told her you weren't my father. But you *are*. You're the man who raised me. You taught me what it means to be a scientist. You taught me what it means to be a person when I could have been a monster so easily. Wake up. For me. Just this once, don't be stubborn, don't be contrary, and wake up."

She kissed his forehead before turning to Alexis.

"It's time," she said. "Start the crank."

Alexis nodded and began turning the vast crank that would open the roof. The two halves of the door slid smoothly open, revealing the cloud-dark sky. Jack flung first one switch, and then another, and another, as the generators engaged, as the air grew thick with ozone and the various machines began to spark and flash.

Lightning lashed down from the heavens, slamming into the lightning rod, filling the windmill with electric light. Jack laughed, high and bright and for one single moment overjoyed, standing in her element and utterly at peace with herself. Alexis smiled, eyes half-closed against the glare.

The lightning faded. Alexis slowly stopped cranking. Jack flipped the switches again, this time pulling them down, cutting off the power.

"Well?" asked Alexis. "Did it work?"

"I don't know," said Jack. "Dr. Bleak?"

On the slab, the dead man—not so dead any longer—opened his eyes.